Nola's Worlds #2

ferrets and ferreting out

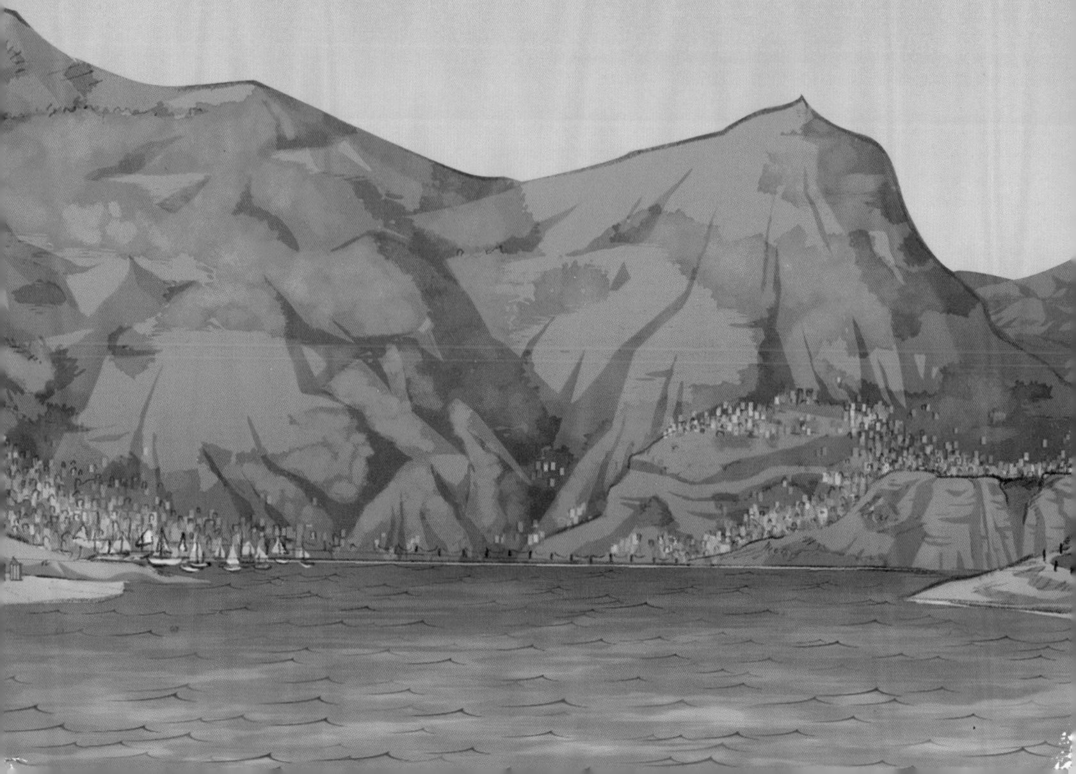

THANK YOU TO KIM AND POP FOR CONTINUING THIS ADVENTURE, WHICH IS STILL JUST AS ENCHANTING. AND A HUGE THANK YOU TO ALICIA AND GAËL, MY LITTLE FERRETS.

TO MARCUS B., JOANNA S., AND HUGO V.,
TO ERIC T. AND STUDIO 5265,
TO FRANCIS H. AND LA COMIX JAM,
THANK YOU TO EVERYONE ♡ FOR THE WELCOME TO MONTREAL.
KARELLE, THANK YOU FOR YOUR HELP WITH THE COLORING. :)

A BIG THANK YOU TO KARELLE AND LÉA FOR THEIR ASSISTANCE AND AN ITTY-BITTY THANK YOU TO KURI FOR HER ITTY-BITTY ASSISTANCE.
THANK YOU TO KIM, TO MATHIEU, AND ESPECIALLY TO GATE AND JAMES FOR THEIR PRICELESS SUPPORT.
AND THANK YOU TO ALL THOSE WHO LOVED BOOK 1.
I HOPE THAT BOOK 2 WILL PLEASE YOU AS MUCH.
HAPPY READING! ^.^

STORY BY MATHIEU MARIOLLE
ART BY MINIKIM
COLORS BY POP
TRANSLATION BY ERICA OLSON JEFFREY AND CAROL KLIO BURRELL

First American edition published in 2010 by Graphic Universe™.
Published by arrangement with MEDIATOON LICENSING — France.

Alta Donna 2 – Furets et fureteuse
© DARGAUD BENELUX (DARGAUD-LOMBARD S.A.) 2009, by Mariolle, MiniKim, Pop.
www.dargaud.com
All rights reserved

Graphic Universe™
A division of Lerner Publishing Group, Inc.
241 First Avenue North
Minneapolis, MN 55401 U.S.A.

Website address: www.lernerbooks.com

Library of Congress Cataloging-in-Publication Data

Mariolle, Mathieu.
   Ferrets and ferreting out / by Mathieu Mariolle ; illustrated by MiniKim ; colored by Pop. — 1st American ed.
      p.   cm. — (Nola's worlds ; #2)
      Summary: As her once perfect and boring hometown Alta Donna becomes increasingly turbulent and dangerous, Nola determines to find the reason and its possible connection to her mysterious new friends Inés and Damiano.
      ISBN 978–0–7613–6504–4 (lib. bdg. : alk. paper)
      1. Graphic novels. [1. Graphic novels. 2. Supernatural—Fiction. 3. Characters in literature—Fiction. 4. Ferrets—Fiction.] I. MiniKim, ill. II. Pop, 1978– ill. III. Title.
   PZ7.7.M34Fer 2010
   741.5'944—dc22   2010012412

Manufactured in the United States of America
2 – MG – 3/1/11

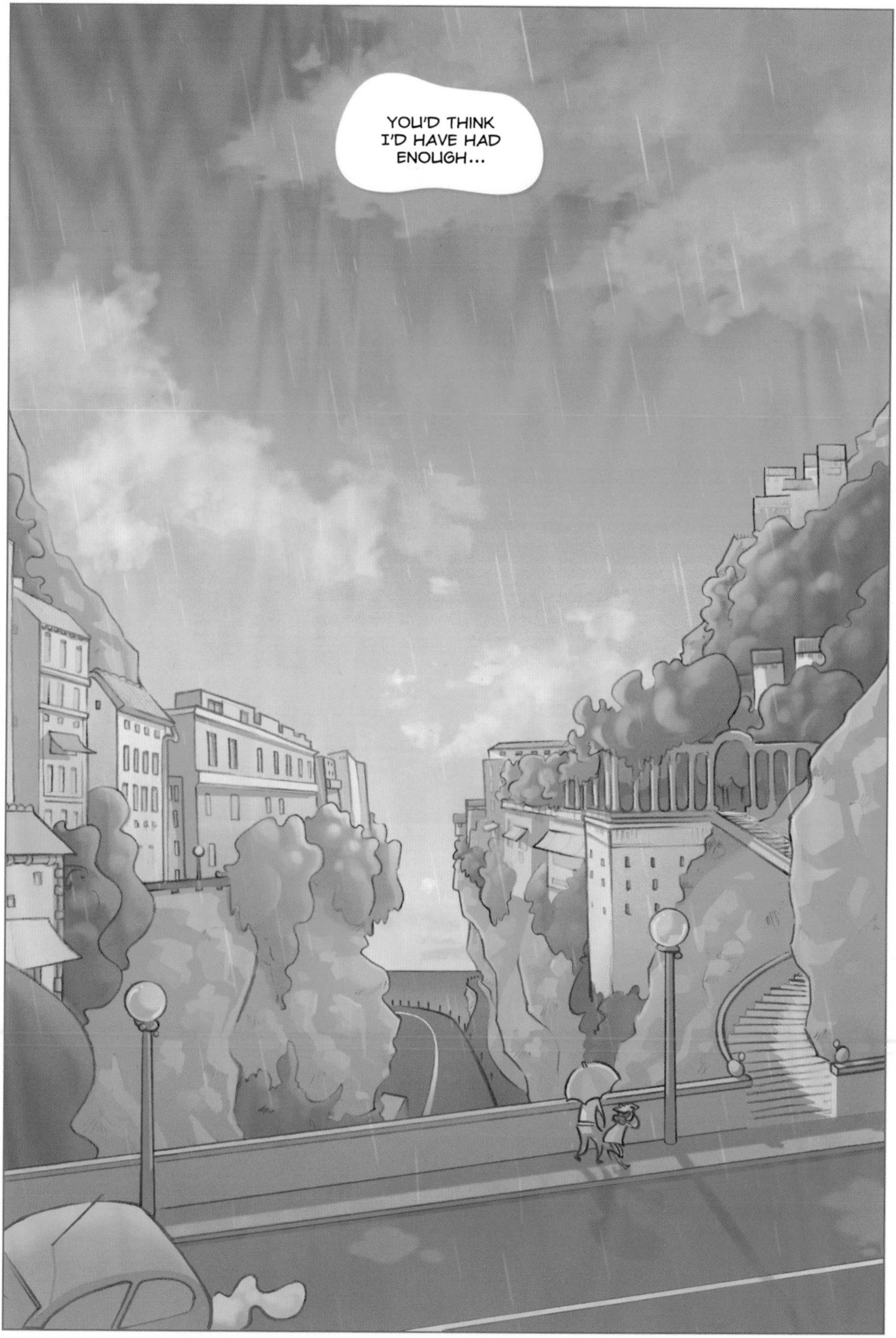
YOU'D THINK
I'D HAVE HAD
ENOUGH...

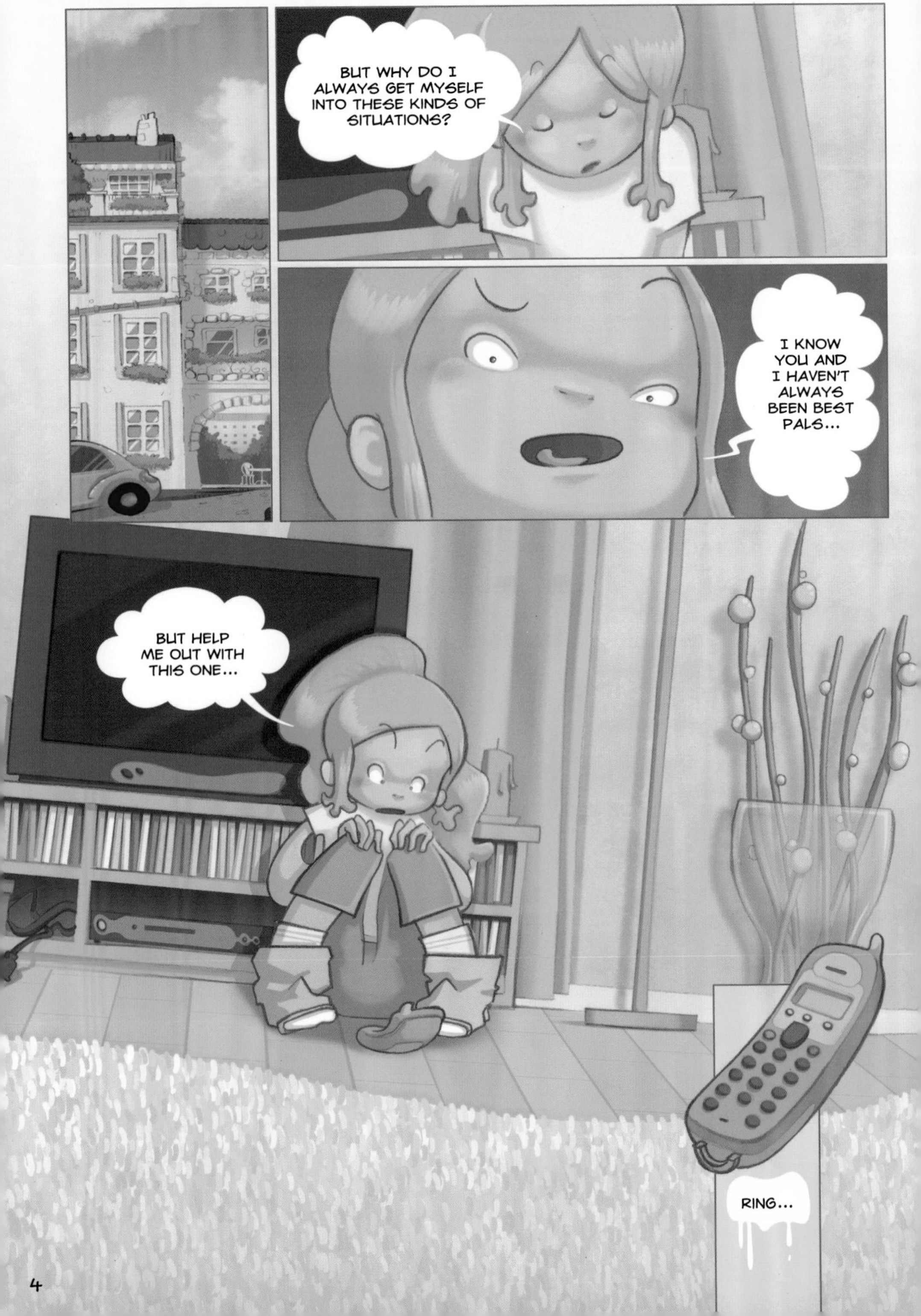

BUT WHY DO I ALWAYS GET MYSELF INTO THESE KINDS OF SITUATIONS?
I KNOW YOU AND I HAVEN'T ALWAYS BEEN BEST PALS...
BUT HELP ME OUT WITH THIS ONE...
RING...

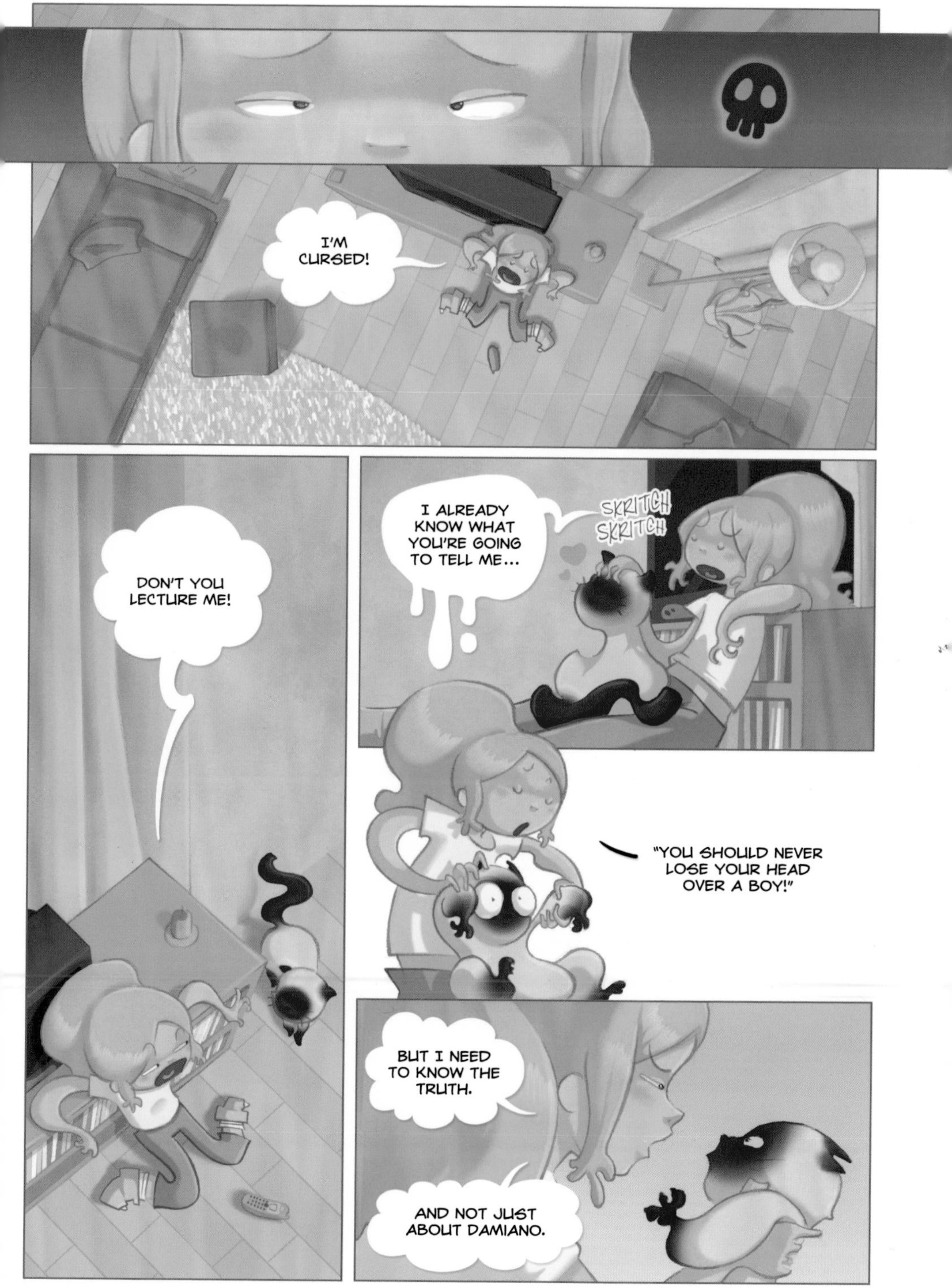
I'M CURSED!
DON'T YOU LECTURE ME!
I ALREADY KNOW WHAT YOU'RE GOING TO TELL ME...
SKRITCH SKRITCH
"YOU SHOULD NEVER LOSE YOUR HEAD OVER A BOY!"
BUT I NEED TO KNOW THE TRUTH.
AND NOT JUST ABOUT DAMIANO.

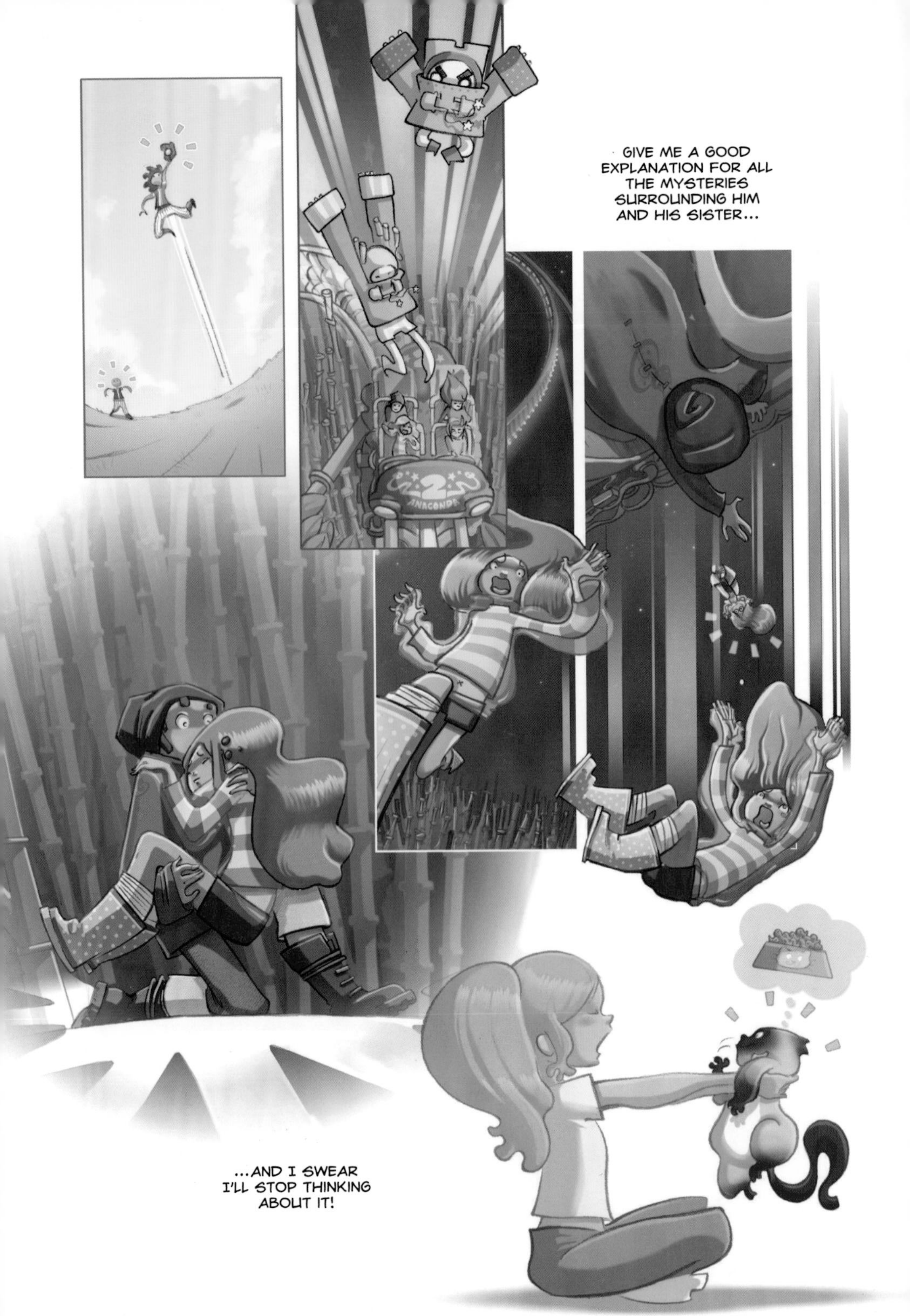

GIVE ME A GOOD EXPLANATION FOR ALL THE MYSTERIES SURROUNDING HIM AND HIS SISTER...
...AND I SWEAR I'LL STOP THINKING ABOUT IT!

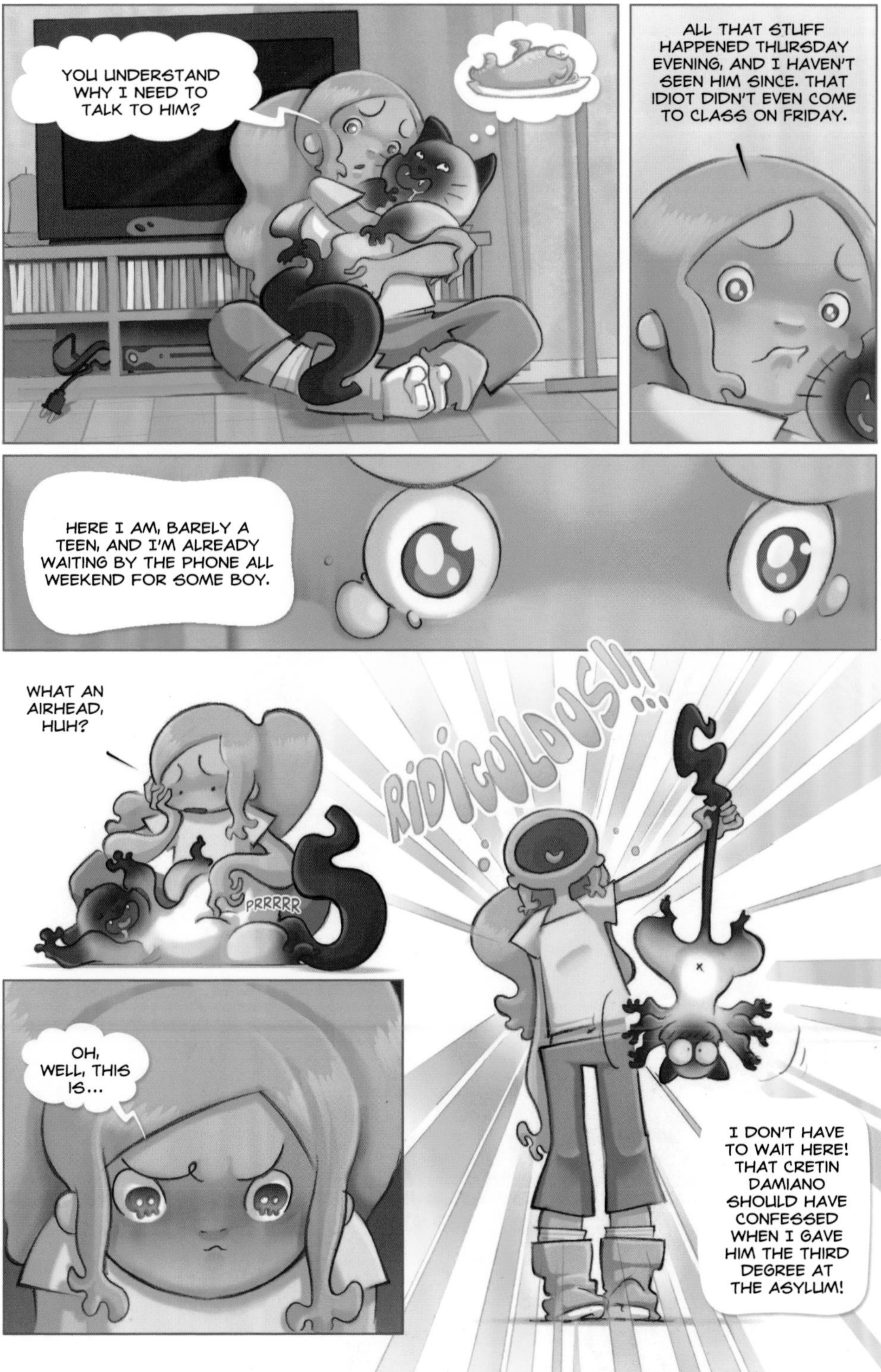
YOU UNDERSTAND WHY I NEED TO TALK TO HIM?
ALL THAT STUFF HAPPENED THURSDAY EVENING, AND I HAVEN'T SEEN HIM SINCE. THAT IDIOT DIDN'T EVEN COME TO CLASS ON FRIDAY.
HERE I AM, BARELY A TEEN, AND I'M ALREADY WAITING BY THE PHONE ALL WEEKEND FOR SOME BOY.
WHAT AN AIRHEAD, HUH?
PRRRRR
OH, WELL, THIS IS...
RIDICULOUS!!!
I DON'T HAVE TO WAIT HERE! THAT CRETIN DAMIANO SHOULD HAVE CONFESSED WHEN I GAVE HIM THE THIRD DEGREE AT THE ASYLUM!

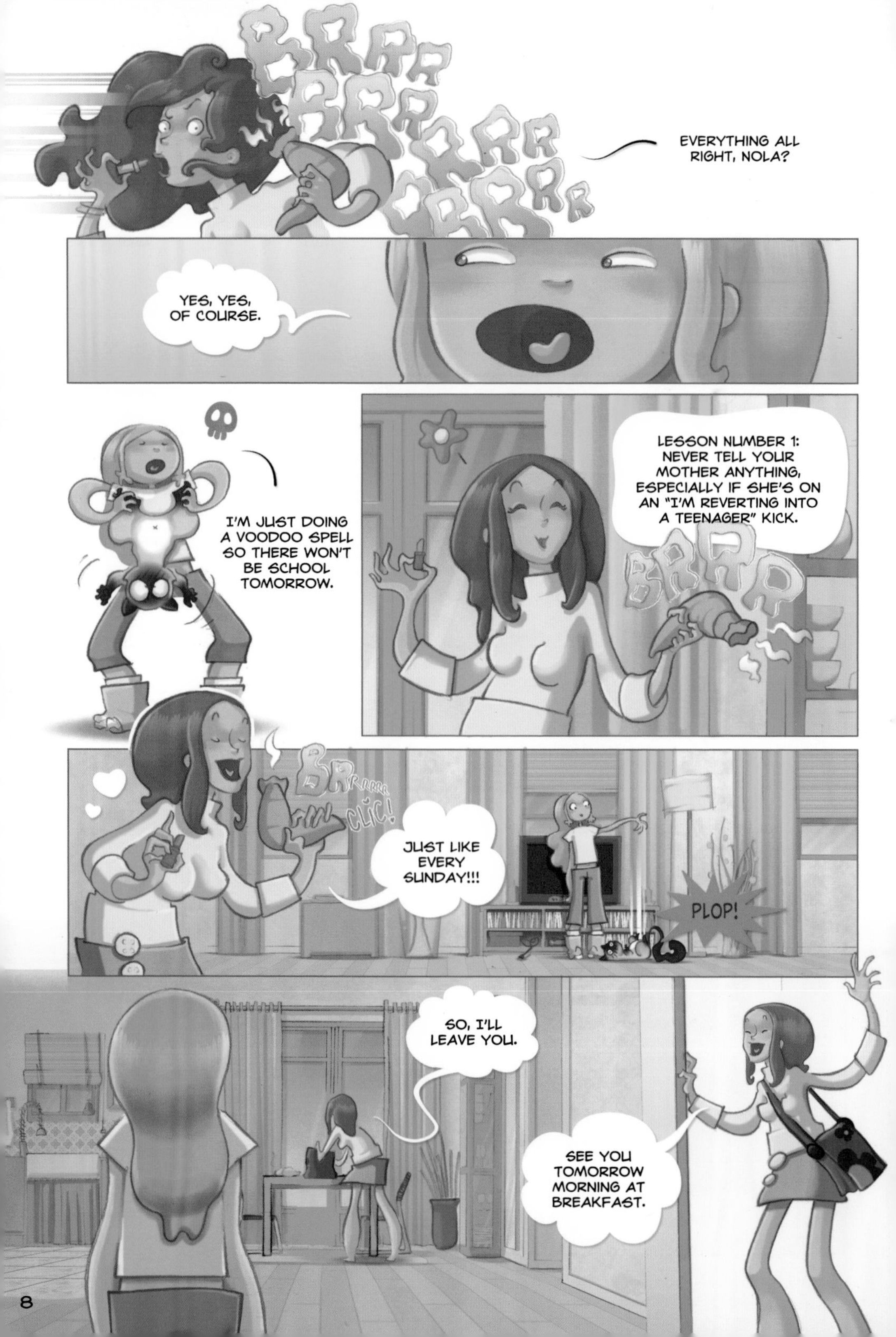
BRRRR BRRRRRR BRRRRR
EVERYTHING ALL RIGHT, NOLA?
YES, YES, OF COURSE.
I'M JUST DOING A VOODOO SPELL SO THERE WON'T BE SCHOOL TOMORROW.
LESSON NUMBER 1: NEVER TELL YOUR MOTHER ANYTHING, ESPECIALLY IF SHE'S ON AN "I'M REVERTING INTO A TEENAGER" KICK.
BRRR
BRrrrrr
CLIC!
JUST LIKE EVERY SUNDAY!!!
PLOP!
SO, I'LL LEAVE YOU.
SEE YOU TOMORROW MORNING AT BREAKFAST.

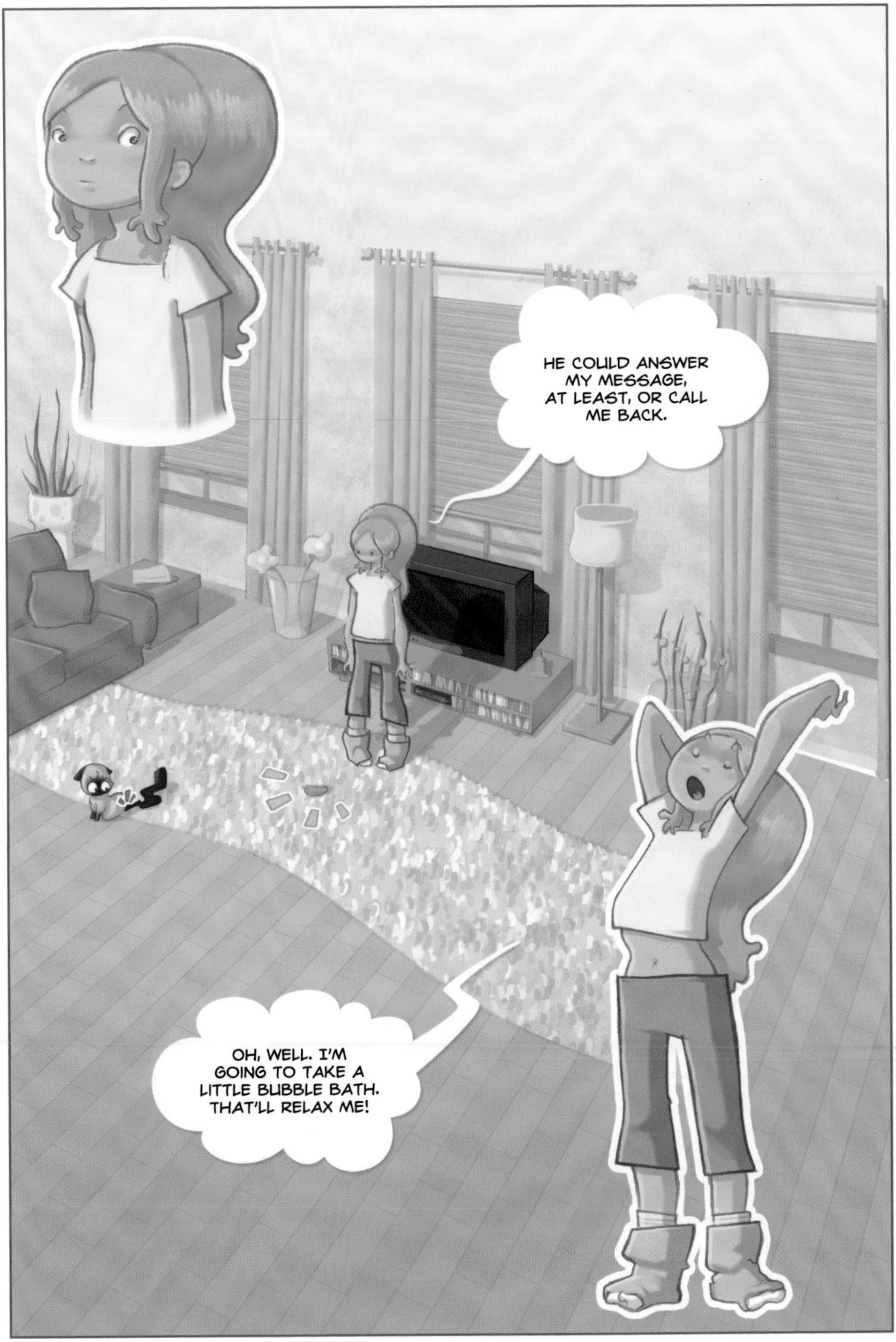
HE COULD ANSWER MY MESSAGE, AT LEAST, OR CALL ME BACK.
OH, WELL. I'M GOING TO TAKE A LITTLE BUBBLE BATH. THAT'LL RELAX ME!

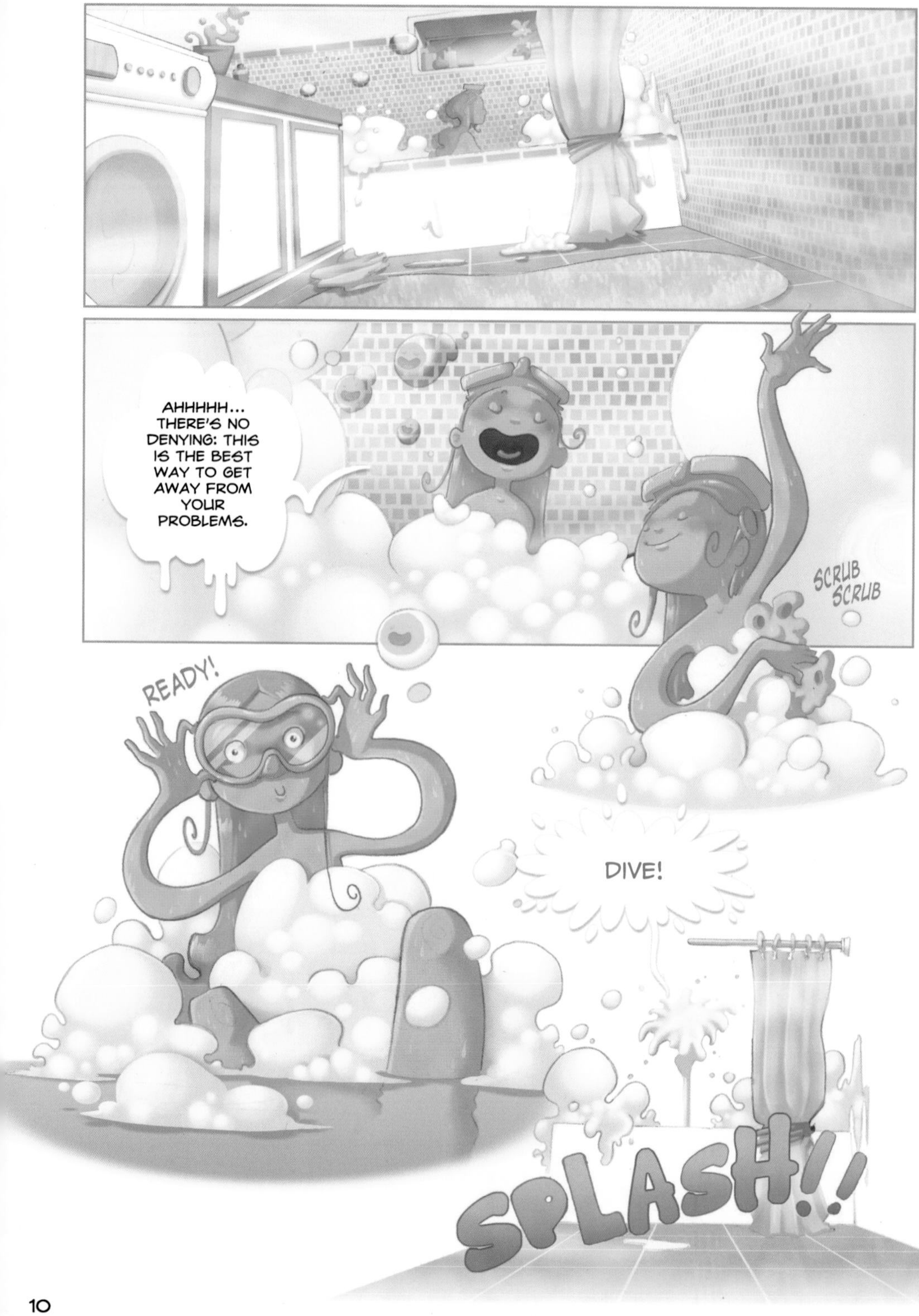

AHHHHH... THERE'S NO DENYING: THIS IS THE BEST WAY TO GET AWAY FROM YOUR PROBLEMS.
SCRUB SCRUB
READY!
DIVE!
SPLASH!!!

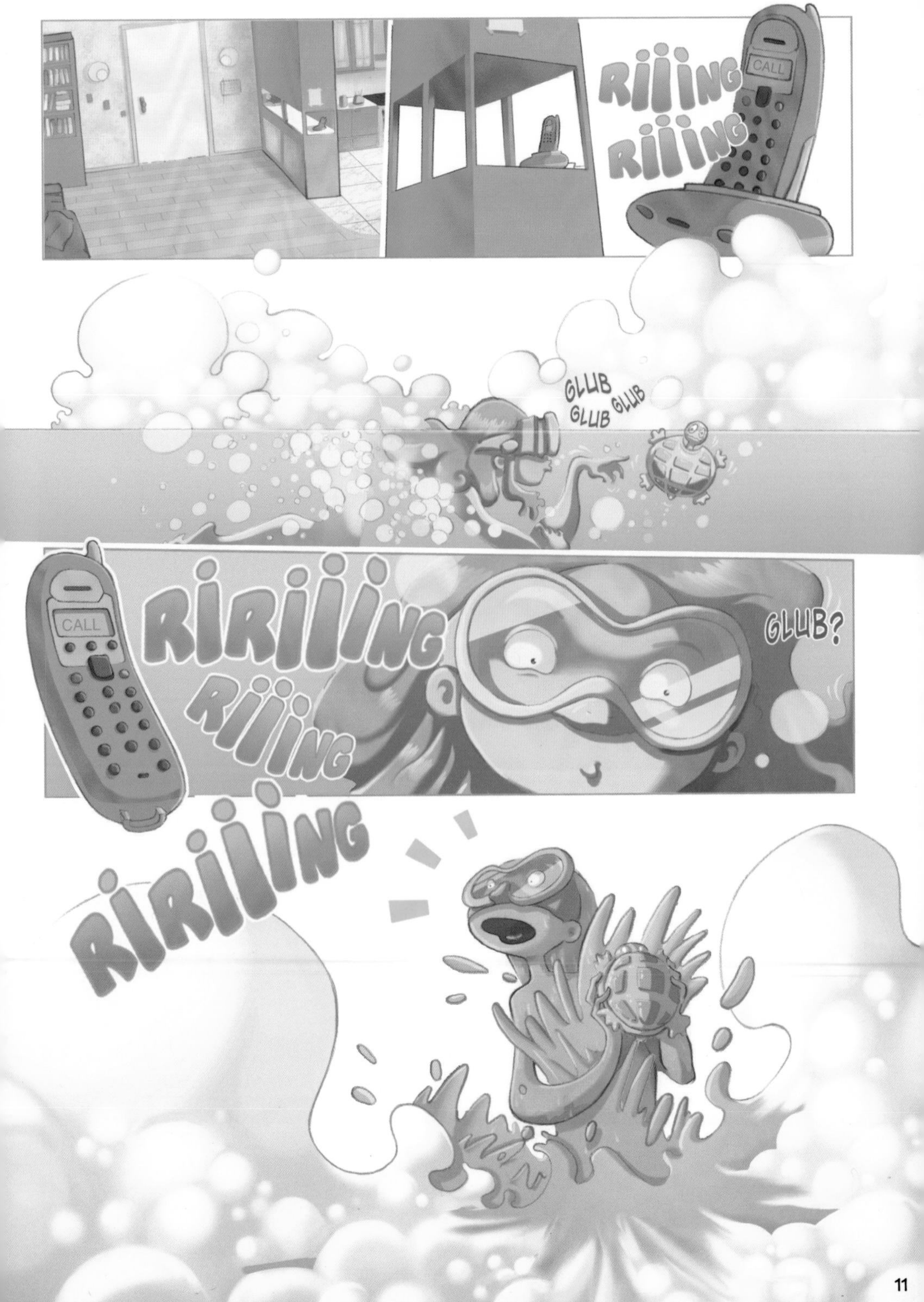
CALL
RIIING
RIIING
GLUB
GLUB
GLUB
CALL
RIRIIING
RIIING
GLUB?
RIRIIING

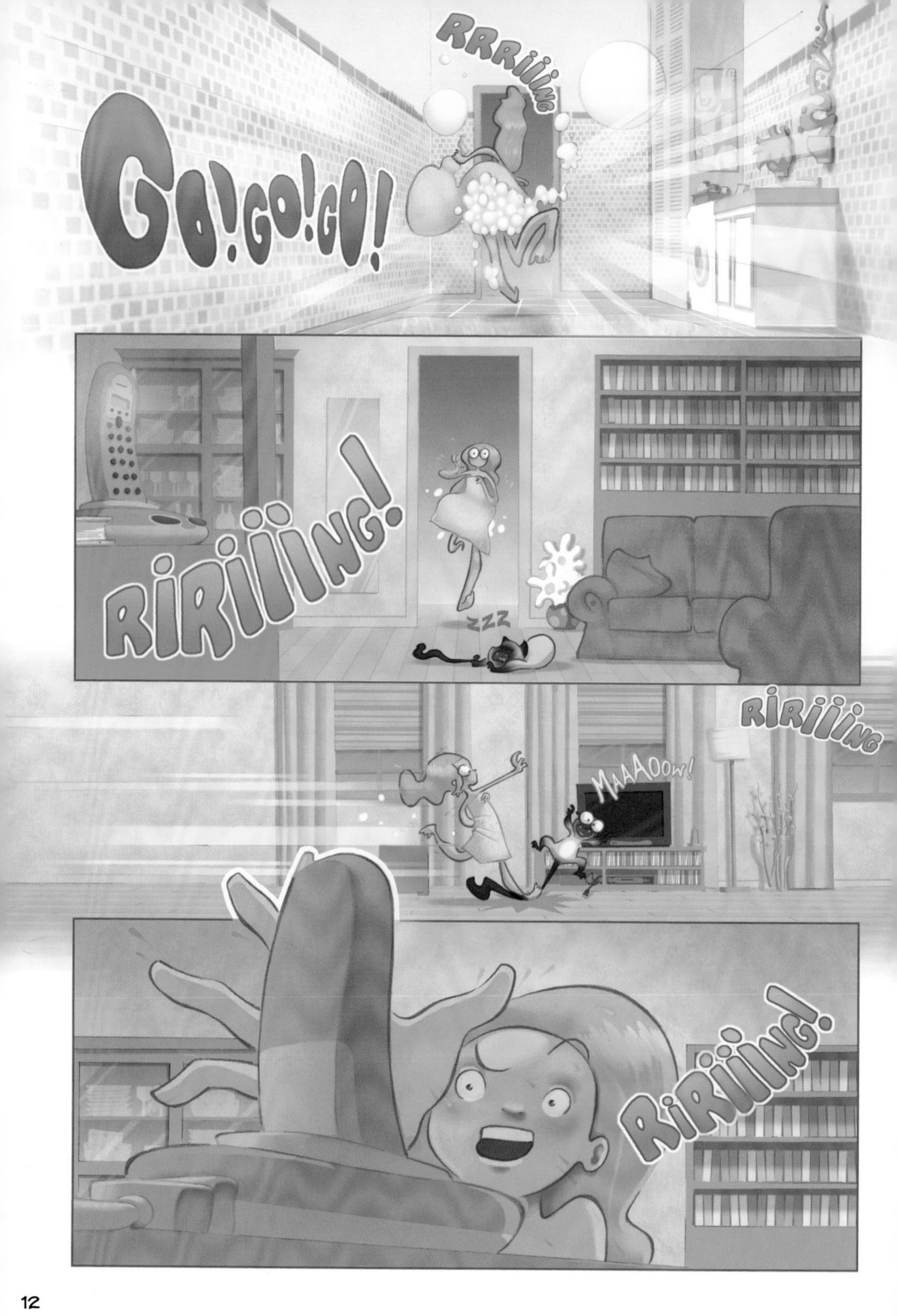
RRRIIIING
GO!GO!GO!
RIRIIIING!
ZZZ
RIRIIIING
MAAAOOW!
RIRIIING!

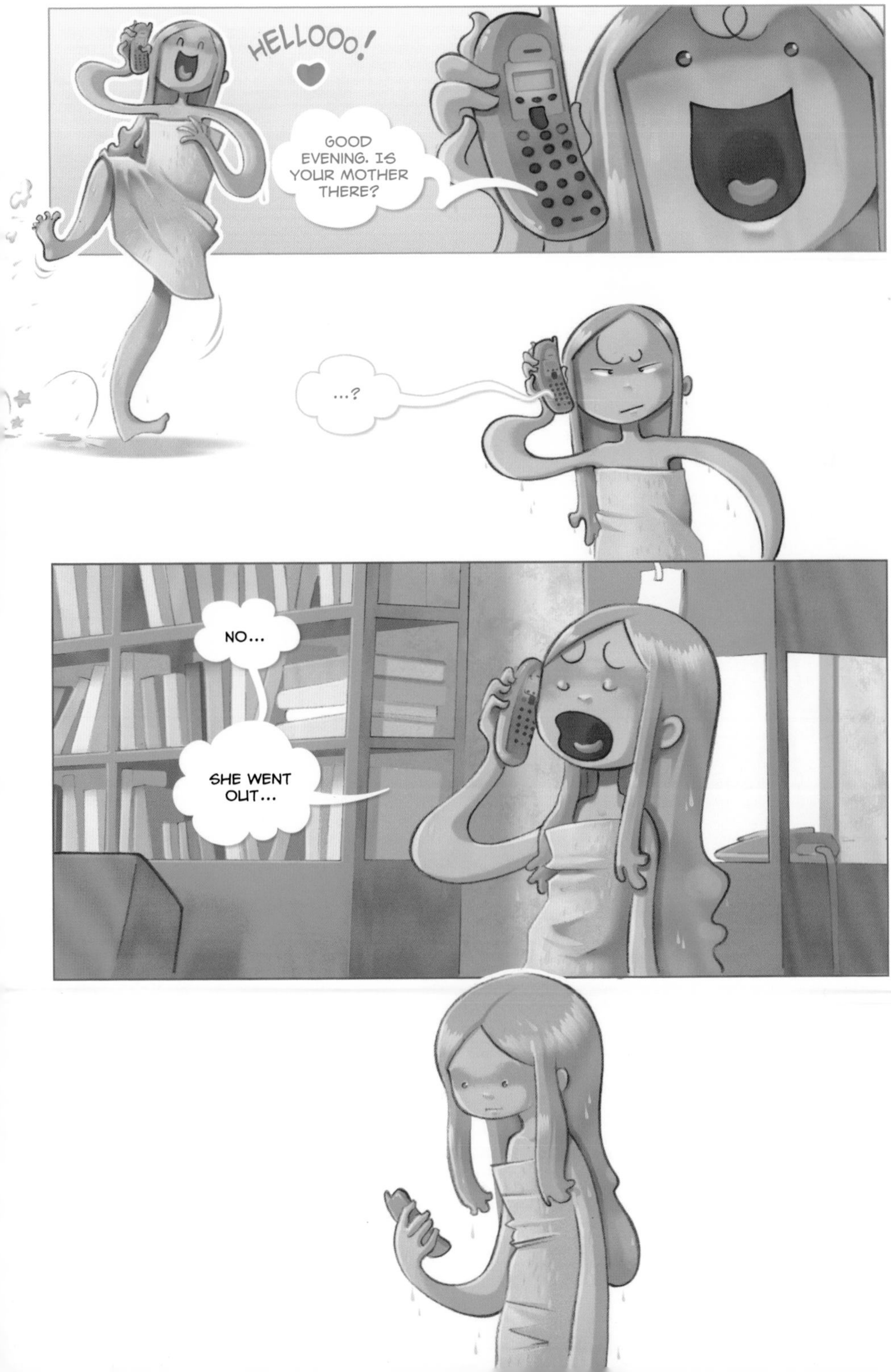
HELLOOO!
GOOD EVENING. IS YOUR MOTHER THERE?
...?
NO...
SHE WENT OUT...

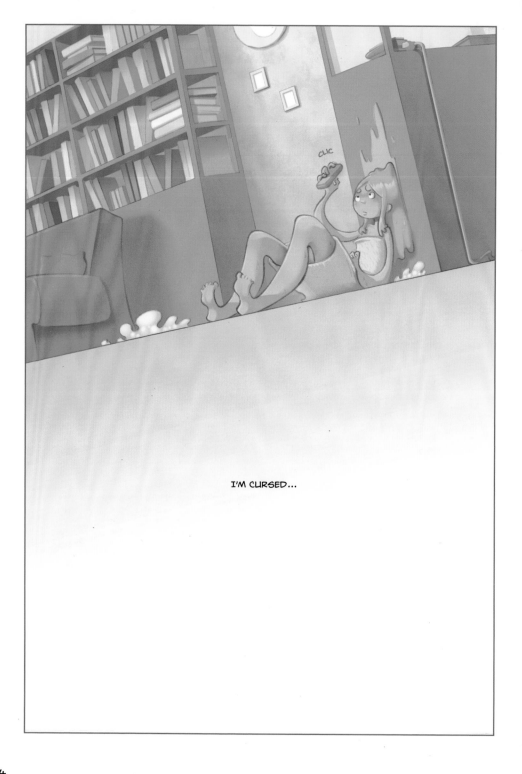

CLIC

I'M CURSED...

Nola's Worlds #2

ferrets and ferreting out

minikim ★ mariolle ★ pop

GRAPHIC UNIVERSE™ · MINNEAPOLIS · NEW YORK · LONDON

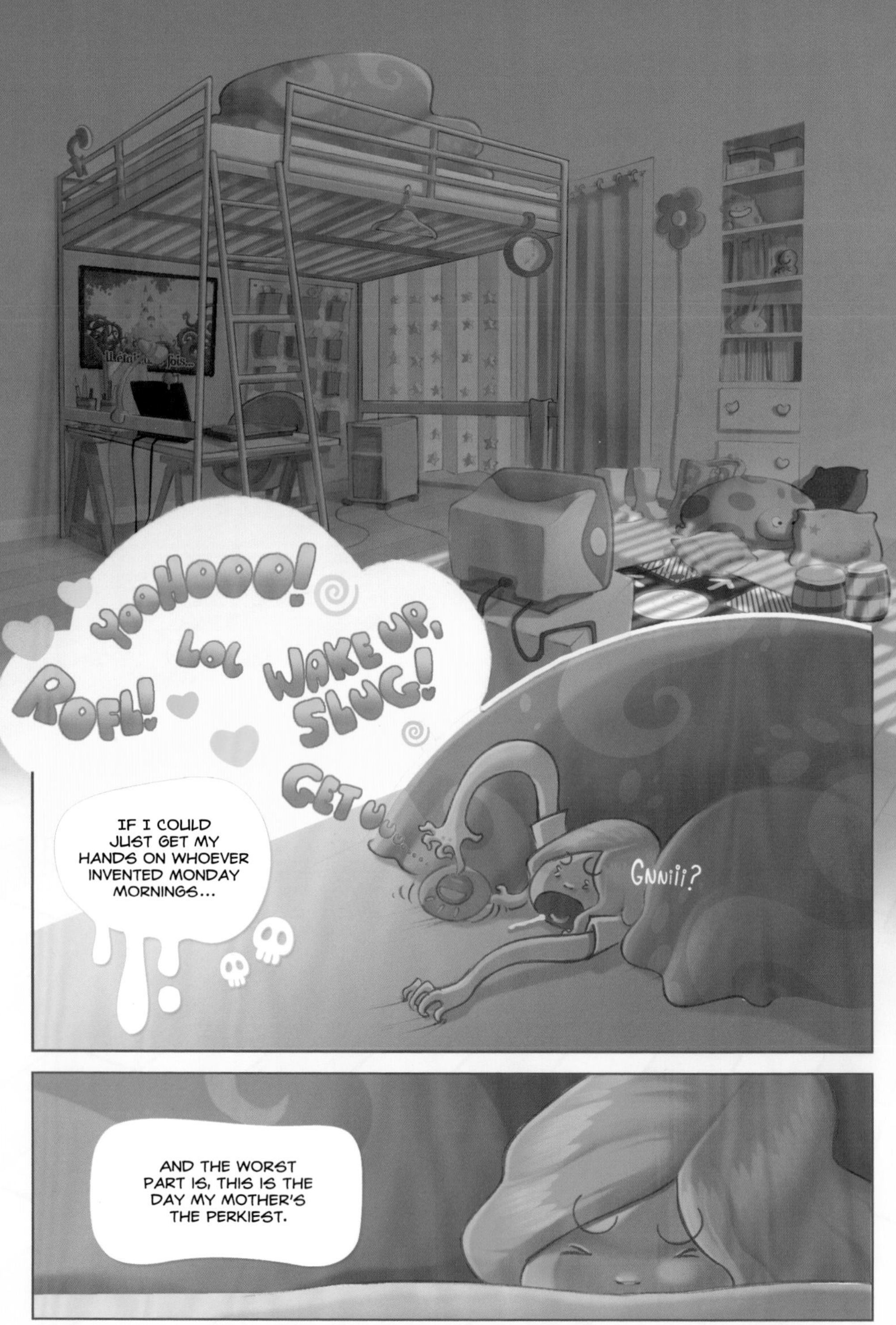
YOOHOOO!
ROFL!
LOL
WAKE UP, SLUG!
GET
IF I COULD JUST GET MY HANDS ON WHOEVER INVENTED MONDAY MORNINGS...
GNNIII?
AND THE WORST PART IS, THIS IS THE DAY MY MOTHER'S THE PERKIEST.

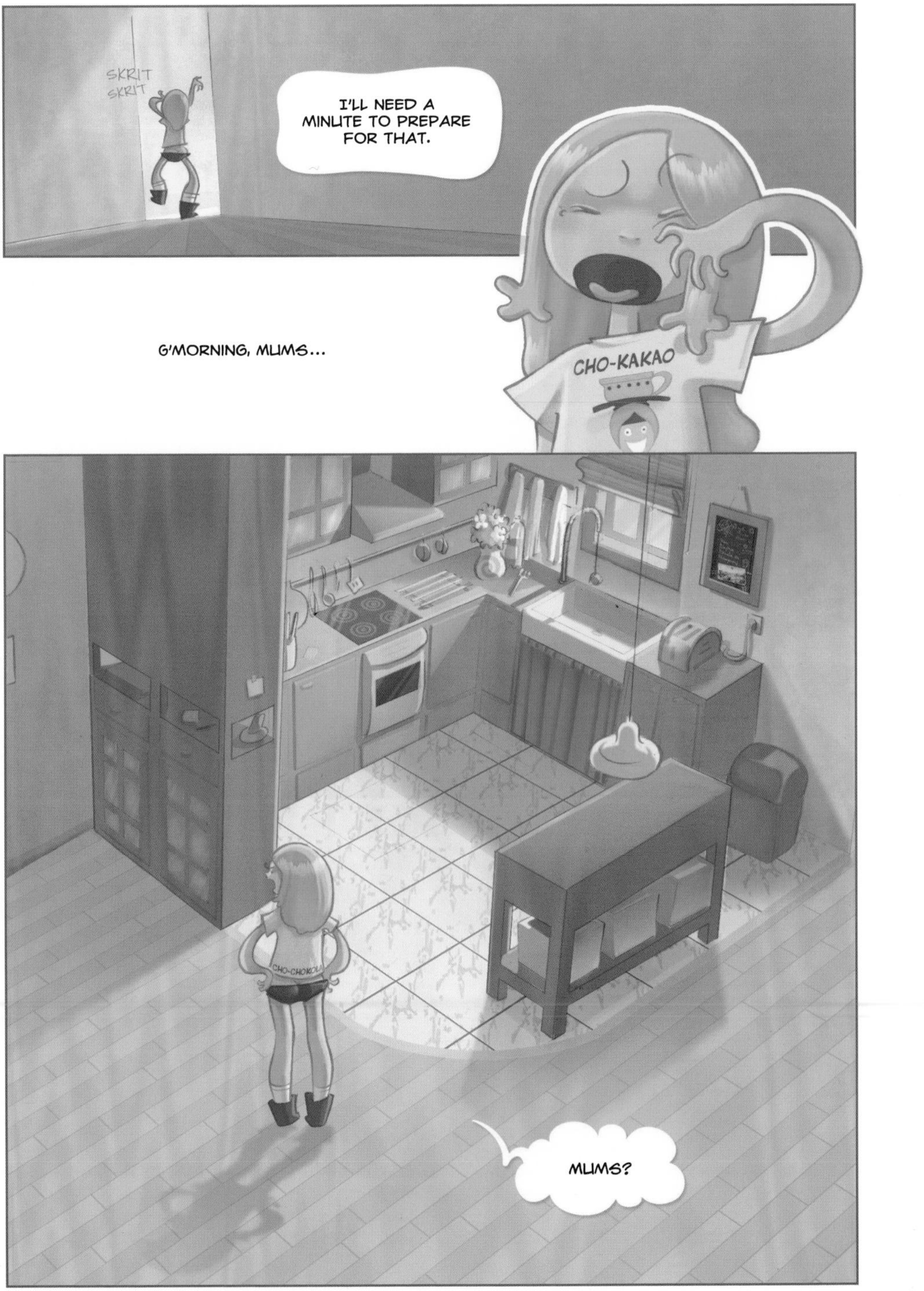
SKRIT
SKRIT
I'LL NEED A MINUTE TO PREPARE FOR THAT.
G'MORNING, MUMS...
CHO-KAKAO
MUMS?

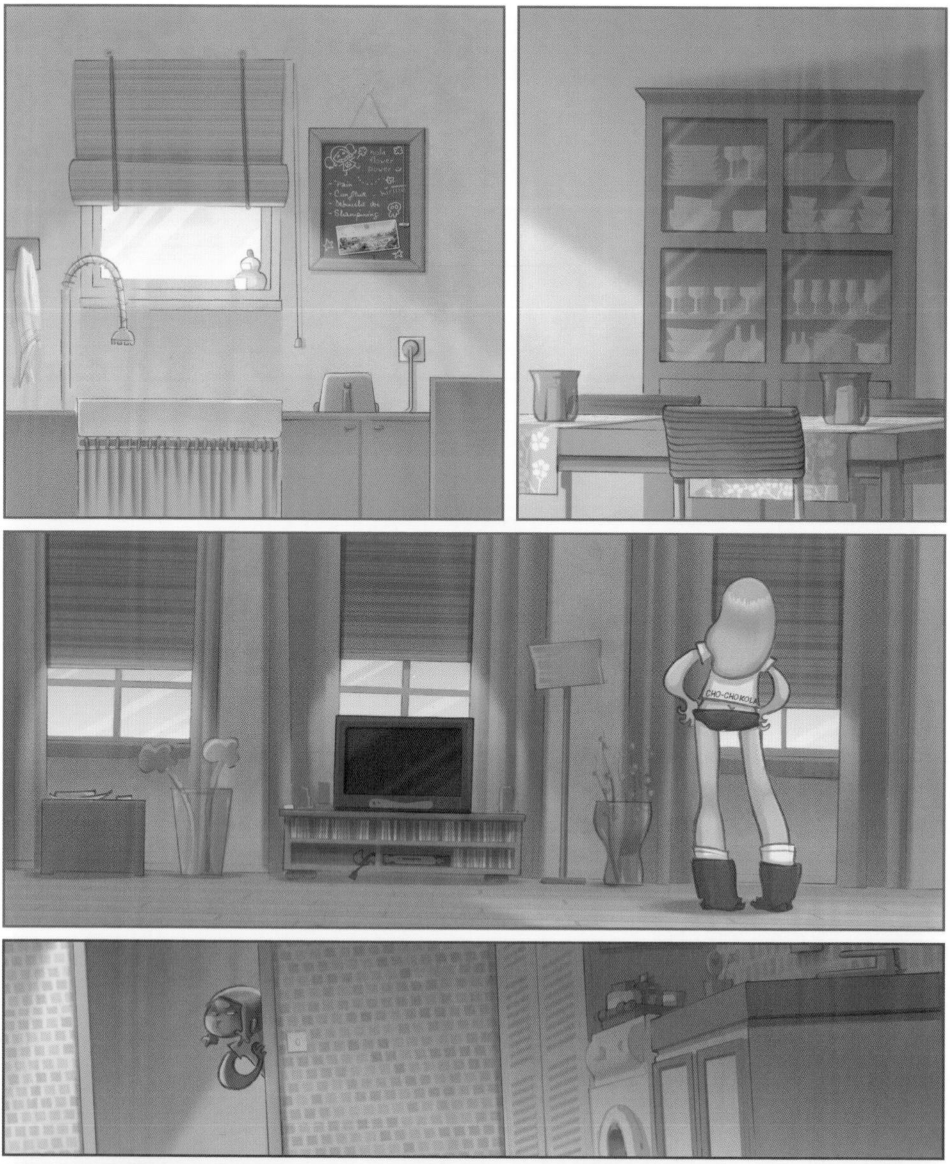
CHO-CHOKOLA
MOTHER?

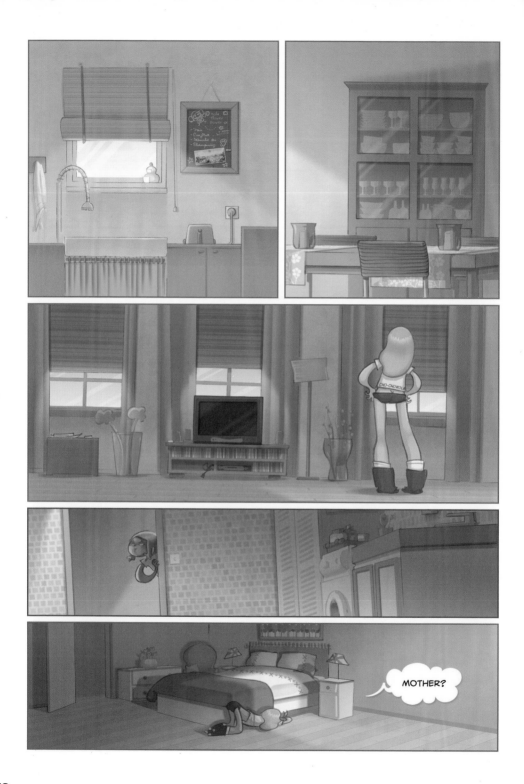

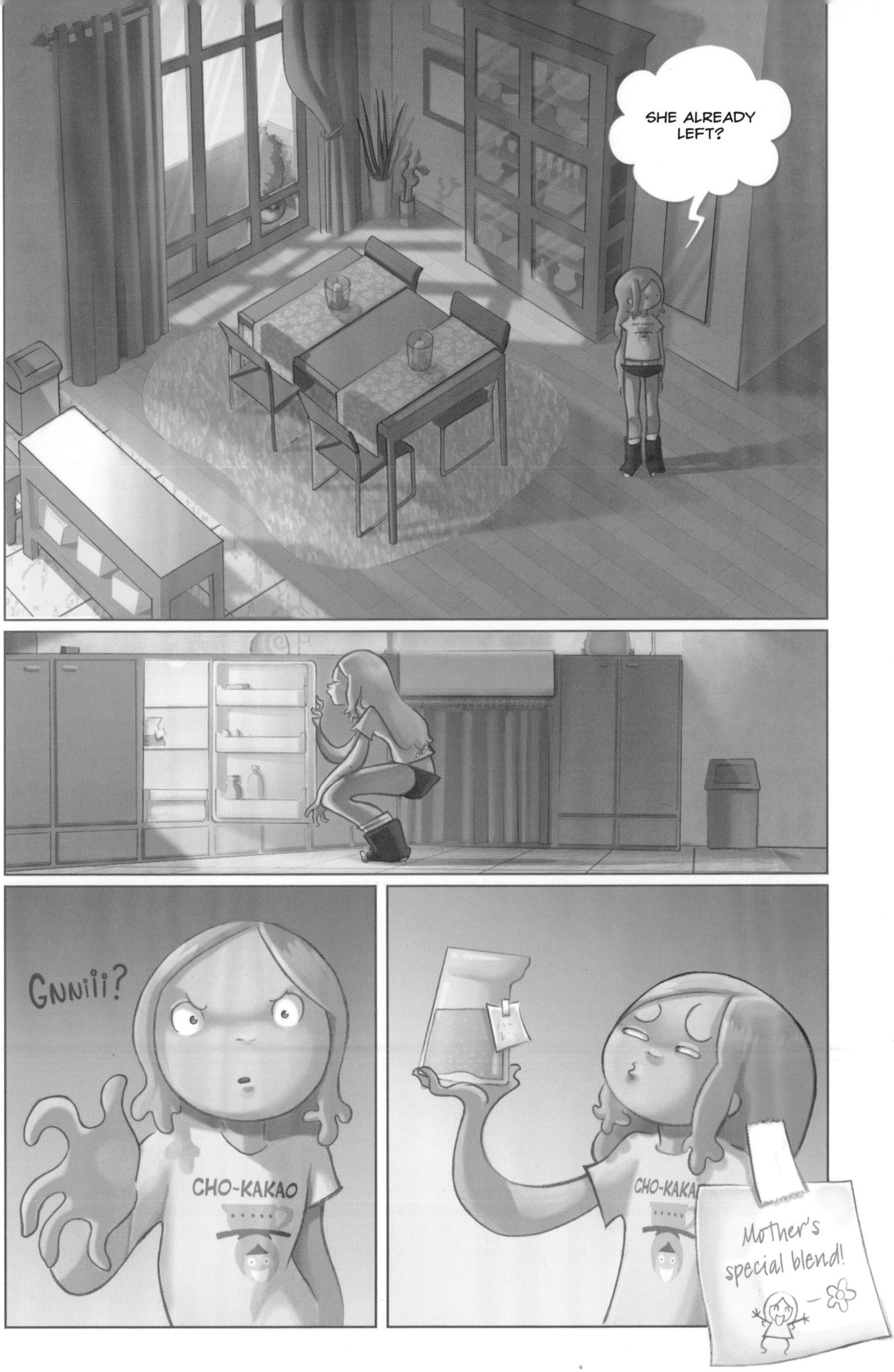

SHE ALREADY LEFT?
GNIII?
CHO-KAKAO
CHO-KAKAO
Mother's special blend!

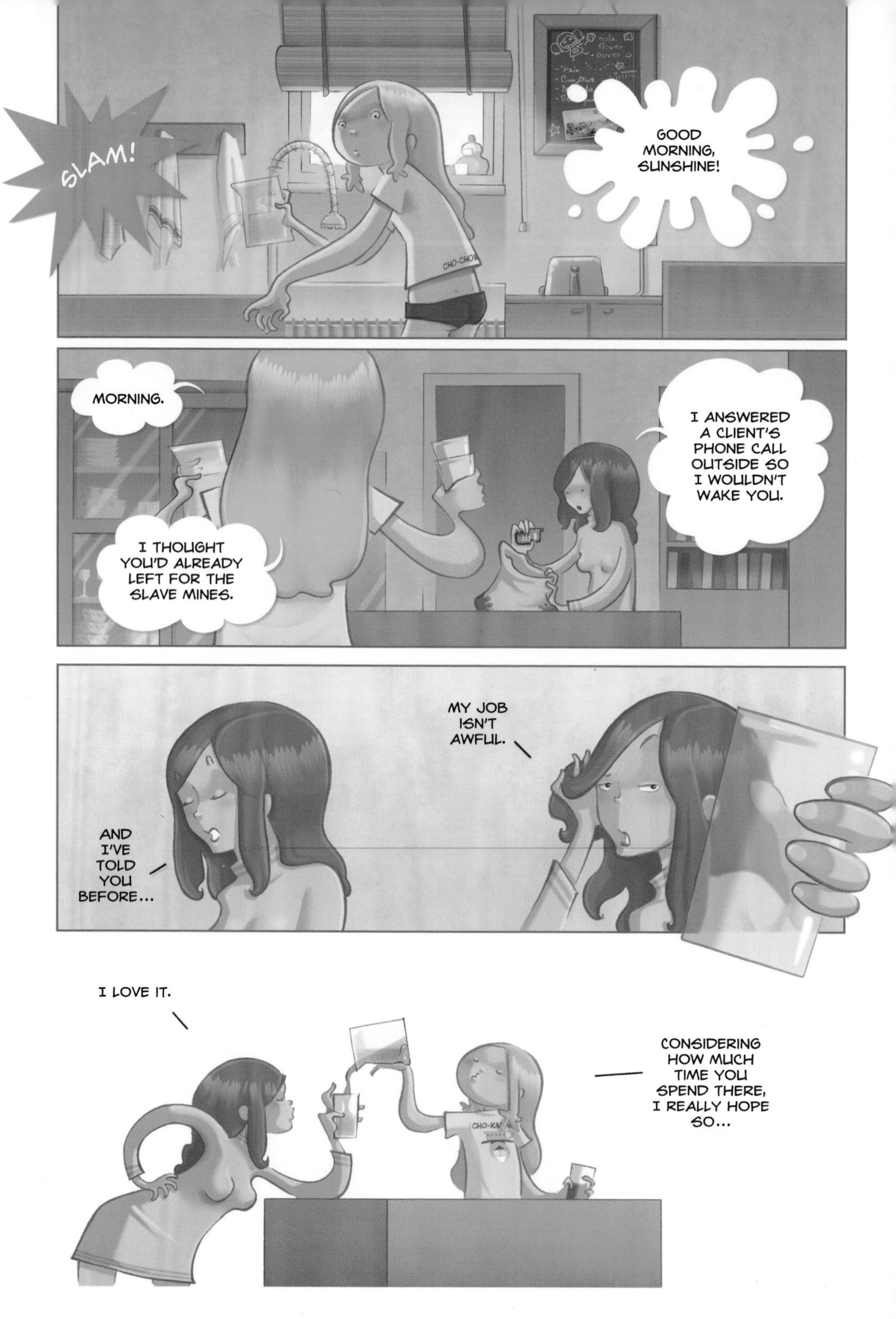
SLAM!
GOOD MORNING, SUNSHINE!
MORNING.
I THOUGHT YOU'D ALREADY LEFT FOR THE SLAVE MINES.
I ANSWERED A CLIENT'S PHONE CALL OUTSIDE SO I WOULDN'T WAKE YOU.
MY JOB ISN'T AWFUL.
AND I'VE TOLD YOU BEFORE...
I LOVE IT.
CONSIDERING HOW MUCH TIME YOU SPEND THERE, I REALLY HOPE SO...

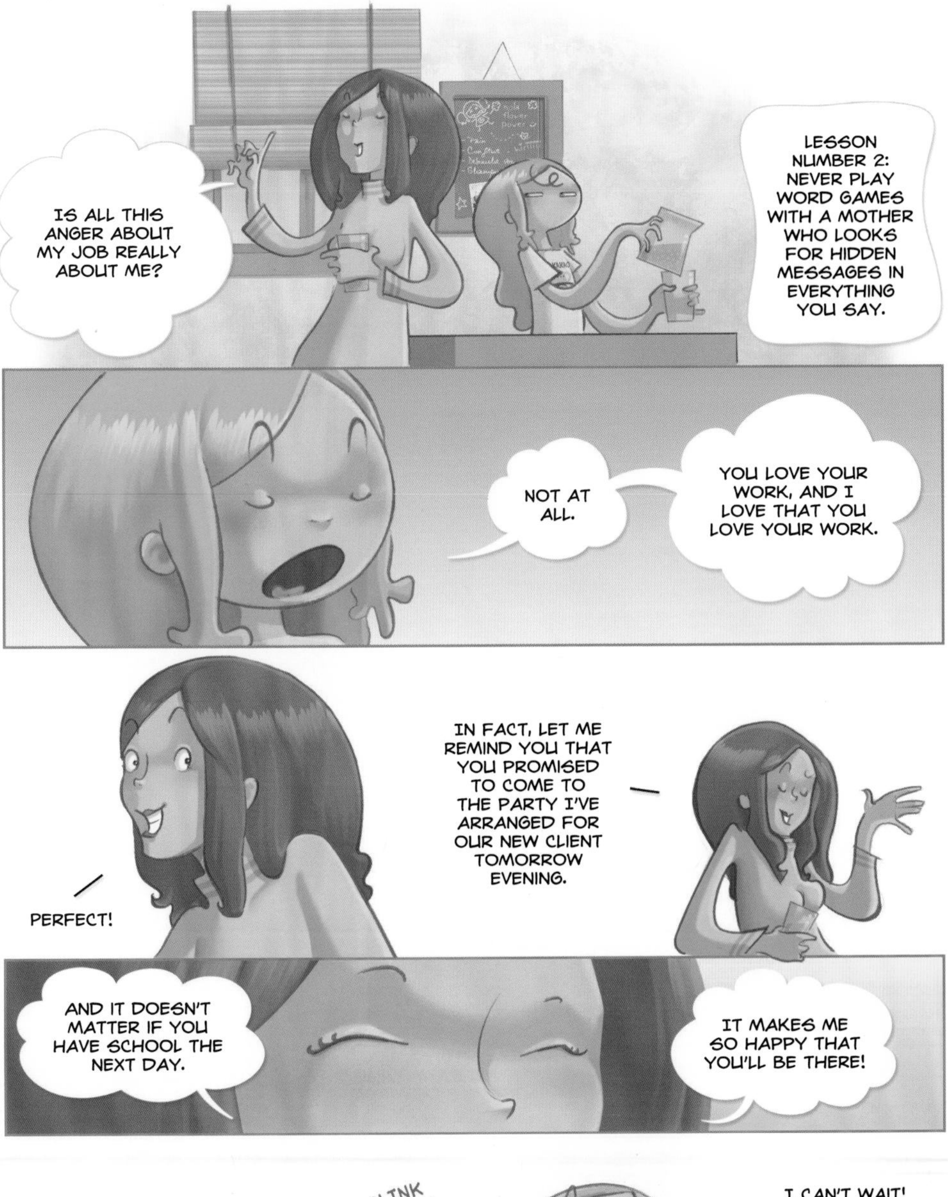
IS ALL THIS ANGER ABOUT MY JOB REALLY ABOUT ME?
LESSON NUMBER 2: NEVER PLAY WORD GAMES WITH A MOTHER WHO LOOKS FOR HIDDEN MESSAGES IN EVERYTHING YOU SAY.
NOT AT ALL.
YOU LOVE YOUR WORK, AND I LOVE THAT YOU LOVE YOUR WORK.
PERFECT!
IN FACT, LET ME REMIND YOU THAT YOU PROMISED TO COME TO THE PARTY I'VE ARRANGED FOR OUR NEW CLIENT TOMORROW EVENING.
AND IT DOESN'T MATTER IF YOU HAVE SCHOOL THE NEXT DAY.
IT MAKES ME SO HAPPY THAT YOU'LL BE THERE!
PLUS, IT'LL BE A CHANCE TO MAKE YOURSELF BEAUTIFUL!
A REAL PARTY FOR A YOUNG LADY!
CLINK CLINK
CHO-KAK
I CAN'T WAIT!

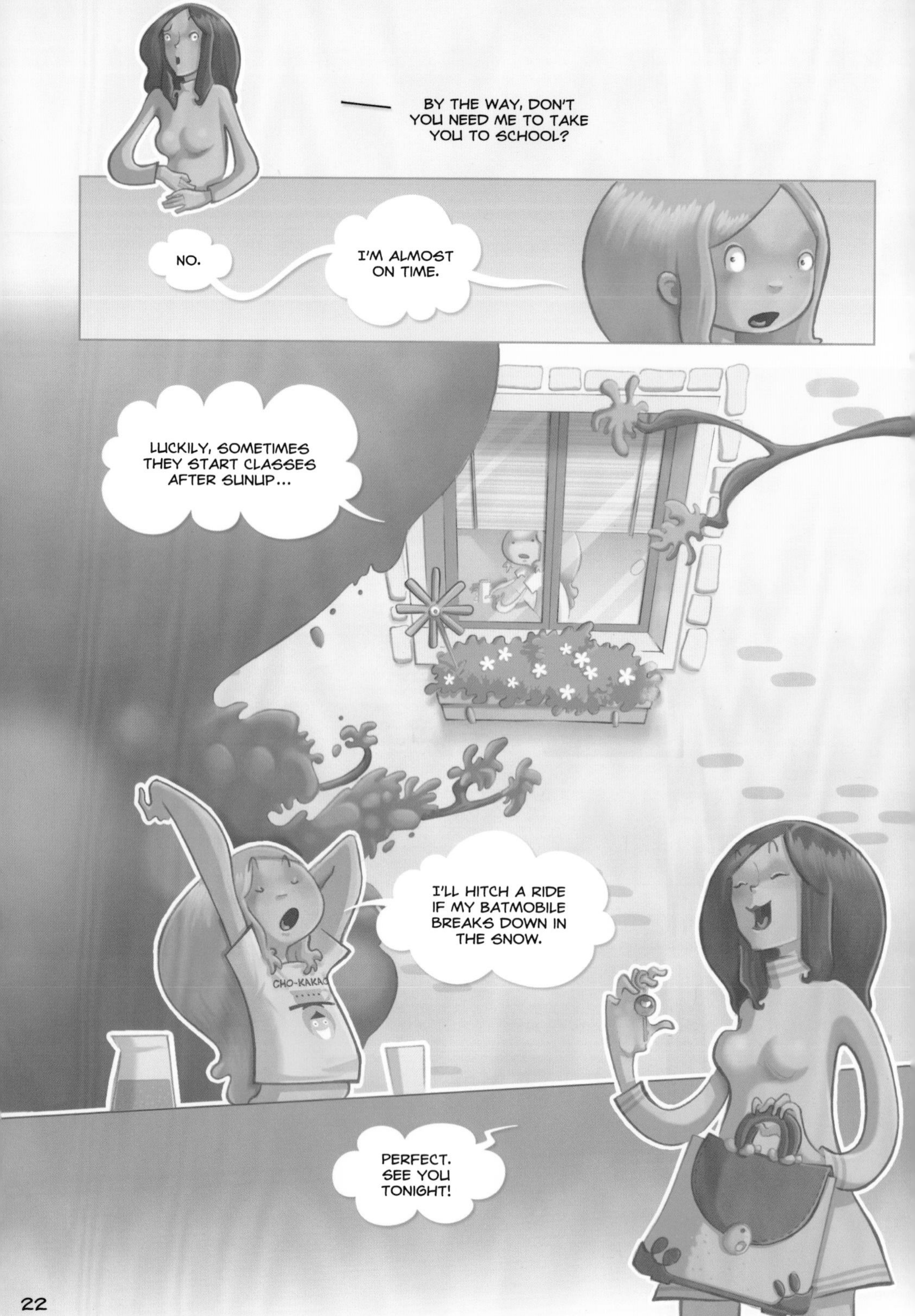
BY THE WAY, DON'T YOU NEED ME TO TAKE YOU TO SCHOOL?
NO.
I'M ALMOST ON TIME.
LUCKILY, SOMETIMES THEY START CLASSES AFTER SUNUP...
I'LL HITCH A RIDE IF MY BATMOBILE BREAKS DOWN IN THE SNOW.
CHO-KAKAO
PERFECT. SEE YOU TONIGHT!

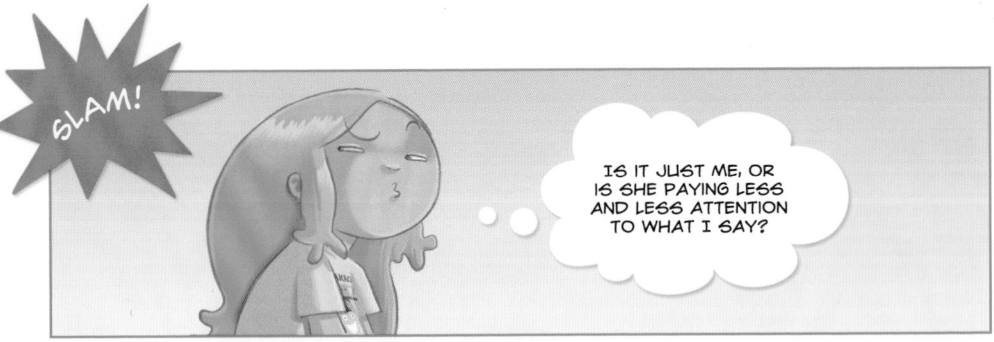
SLAM!
IS IT JUST ME, OR IS SHE PAYING LESS AND LESS ATTENTION TO WHAT I SAY?

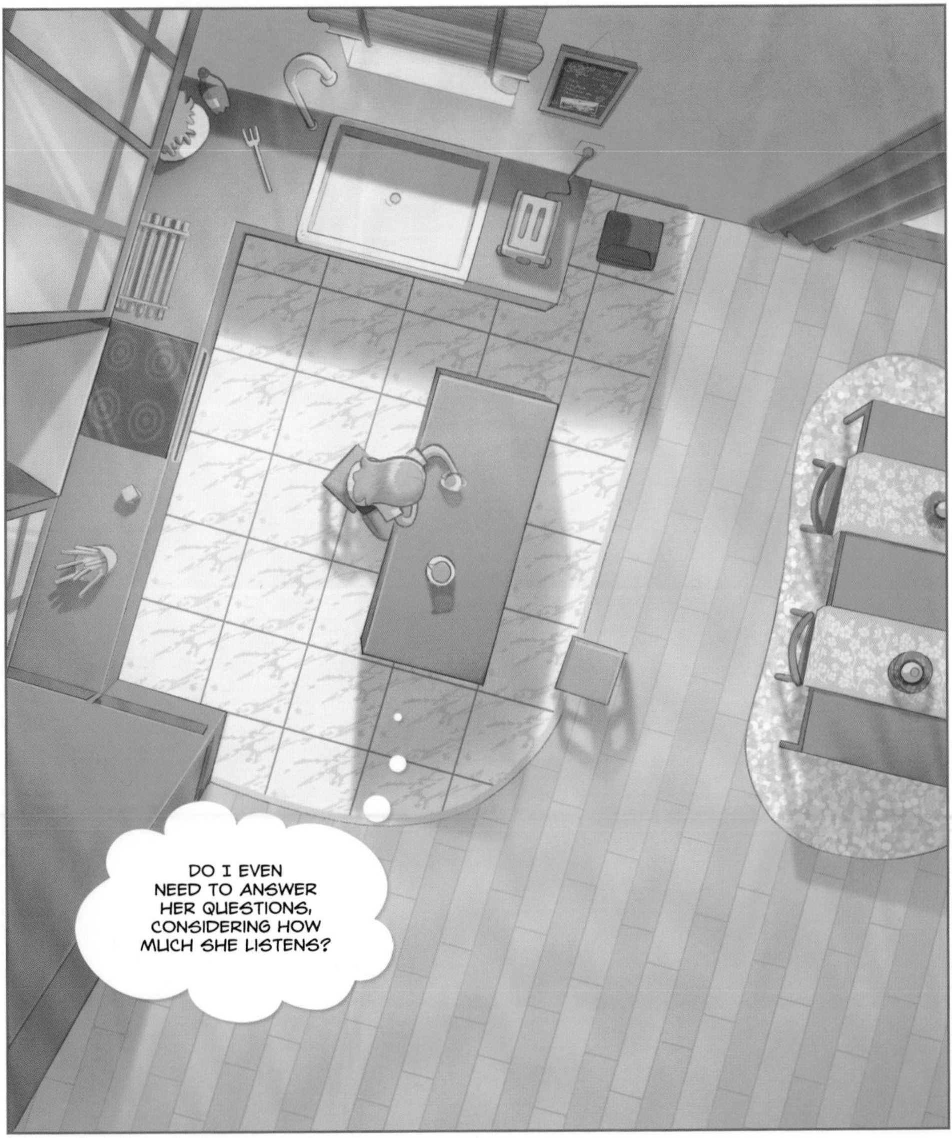
DO I EVEN NEED TO ANSWER HER QUESTIONS, CONSIDERING HOW MUCH SHE LISTENS?

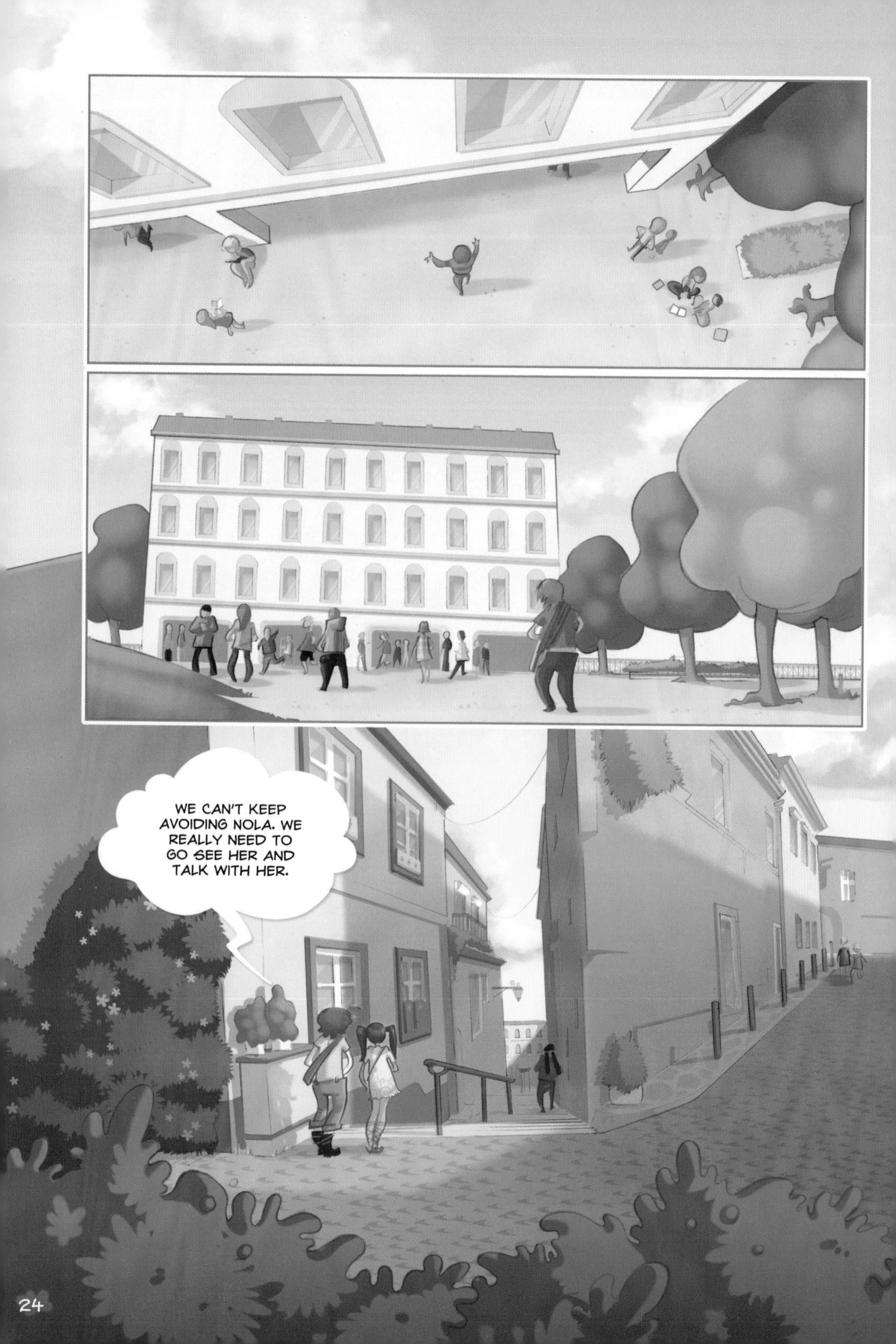
WE CAN'T KEEP AVOIDING NOLA. WE REALLY NEED TO GO SEE HER AND TALK WITH HER.

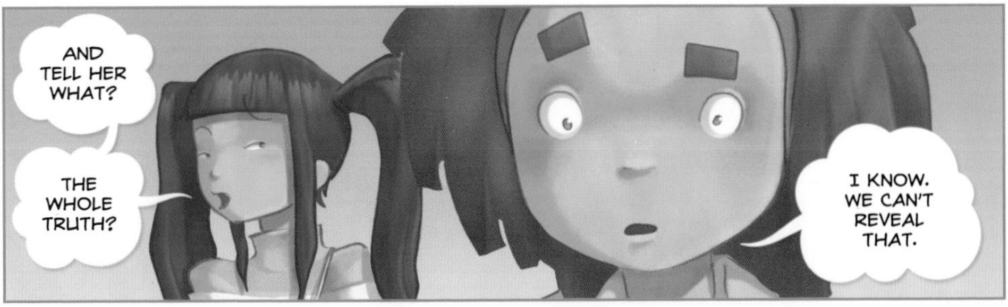
AND TELL HER WHAT?
THE WHOLE TRUTH?
I KNOW. WE CAN'T REVEAL THAT.

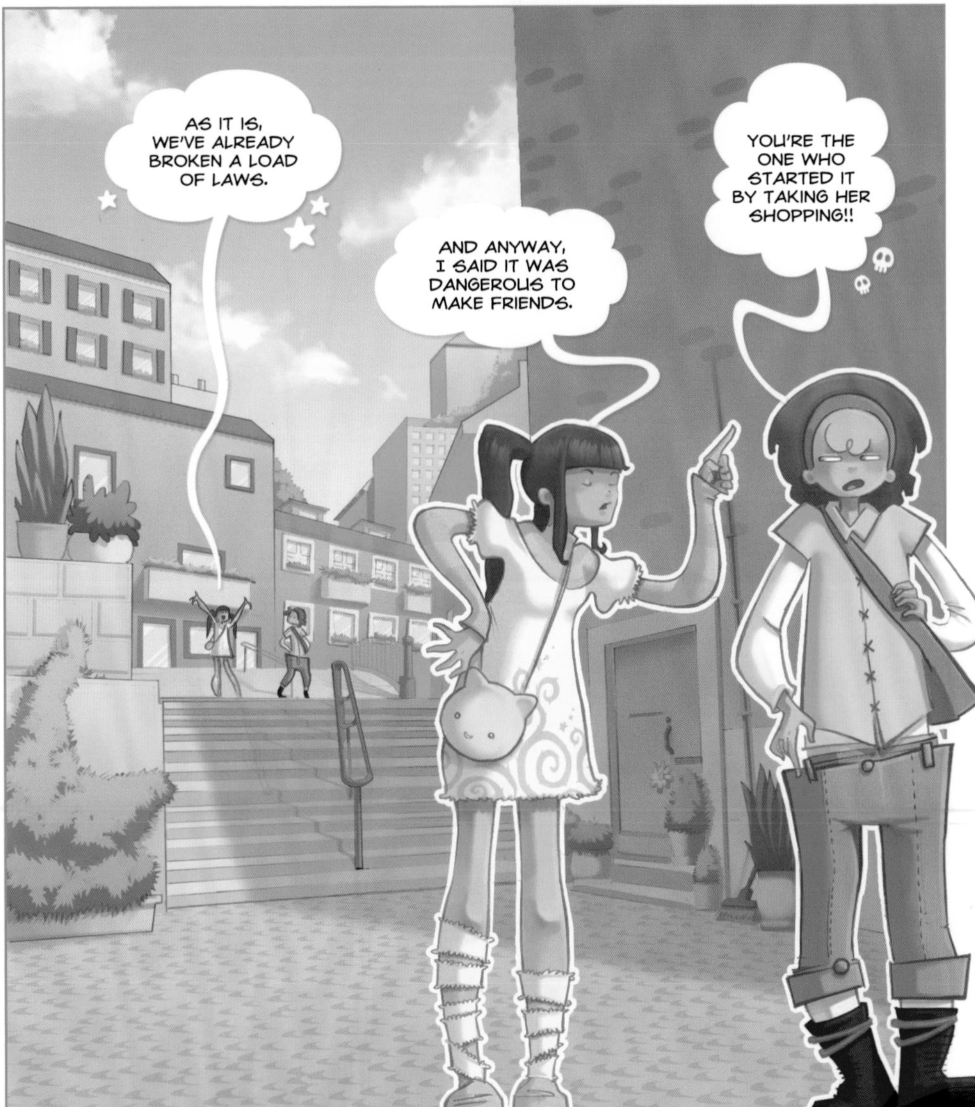
AS IT IS, WE'VE ALREADY BROKEN A LOAD OF LAWS.
AND ANYWAY, I SAID IT WAS DANGEROUS TO MAKE FRIENDS.
YOU'RE THE ONE WHO STARTED IT BY TAKING HER SHOPPING!!

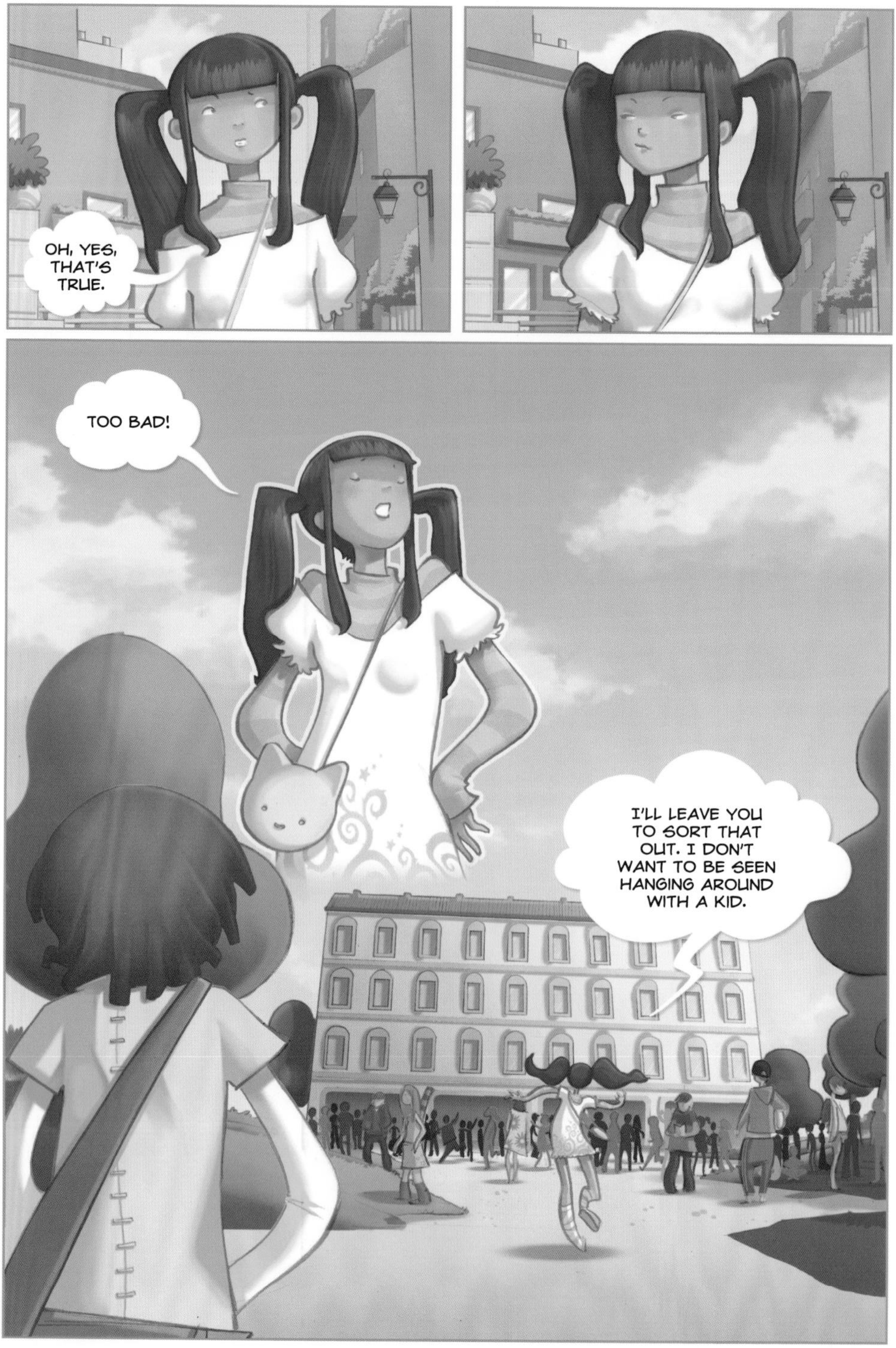
OH, YES, THAT'S TRUE.
TOO BAD!
I'LL LEAVE YOU TO SORT THAT OUT. I DON'T WANT TO BE SEEN HANGING AROUND WITH A KID.

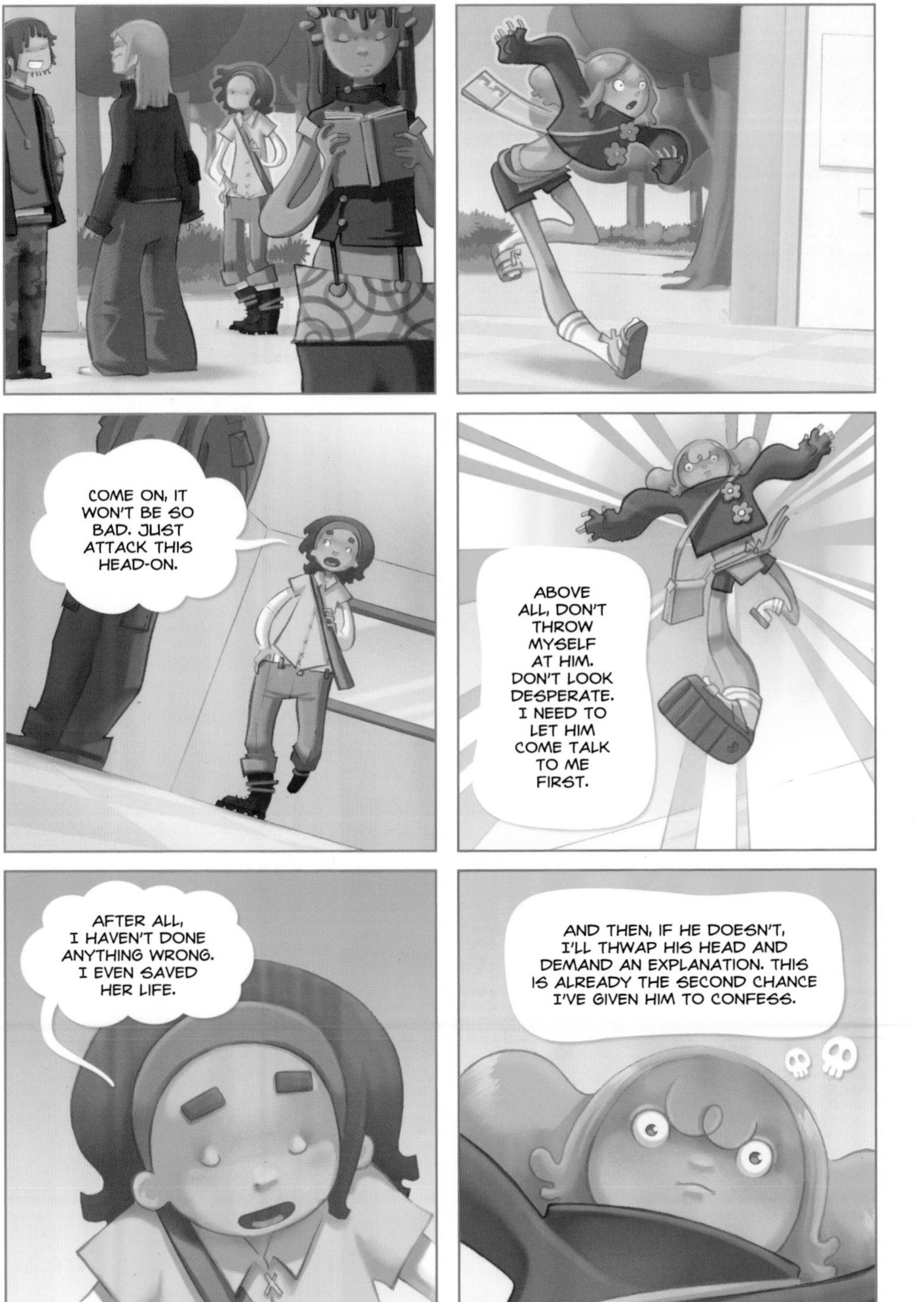
COME ON, IT WON'T BE SO BAD. JUST ATTACK THIS HEAD-ON.
ABOVE ALL, DON'T THROW MYSELF AT HIM. DON'T LOOK DESPERATE. I NEED TO LET HIM COME TALK TO ME FIRST.
AFTER ALL, I HAVEN'T DONE ANYTHING WRONG. I EVEN SAVED HER LIFE.
AND THEN, IF HE DOESN'T, I'LL THWAP HIS HEAD AND DEMAND AN EXPLANATION. THIS IS ALREADY THE SECOND CHANCE I'VE GIVEN HIM TO CONFESS.

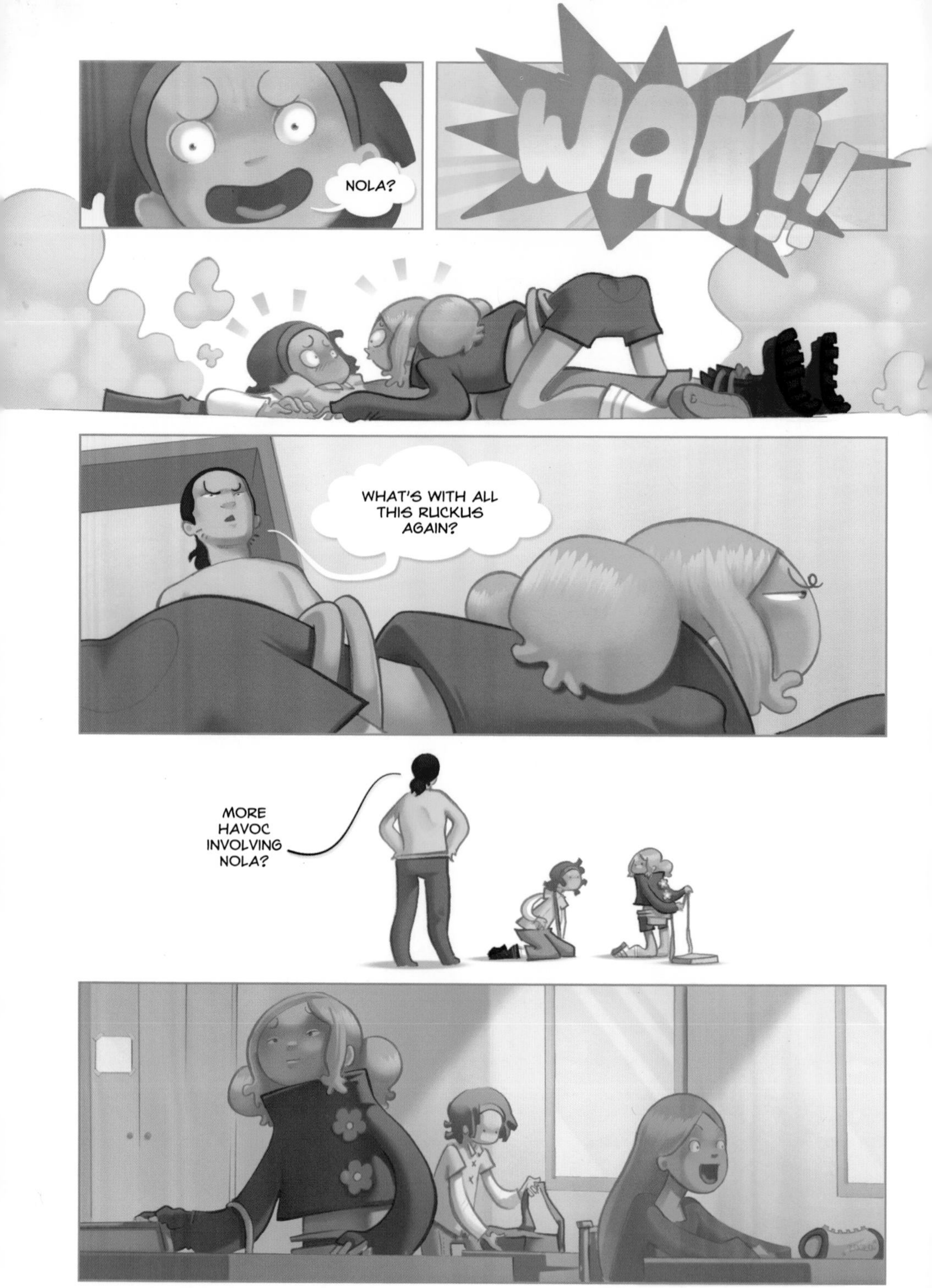
NOLA?
WAK!!!
WHAT'S WITH ALL THIS RUCKUS AGAIN?
MORE HAVOC INVOLVING NOLA?

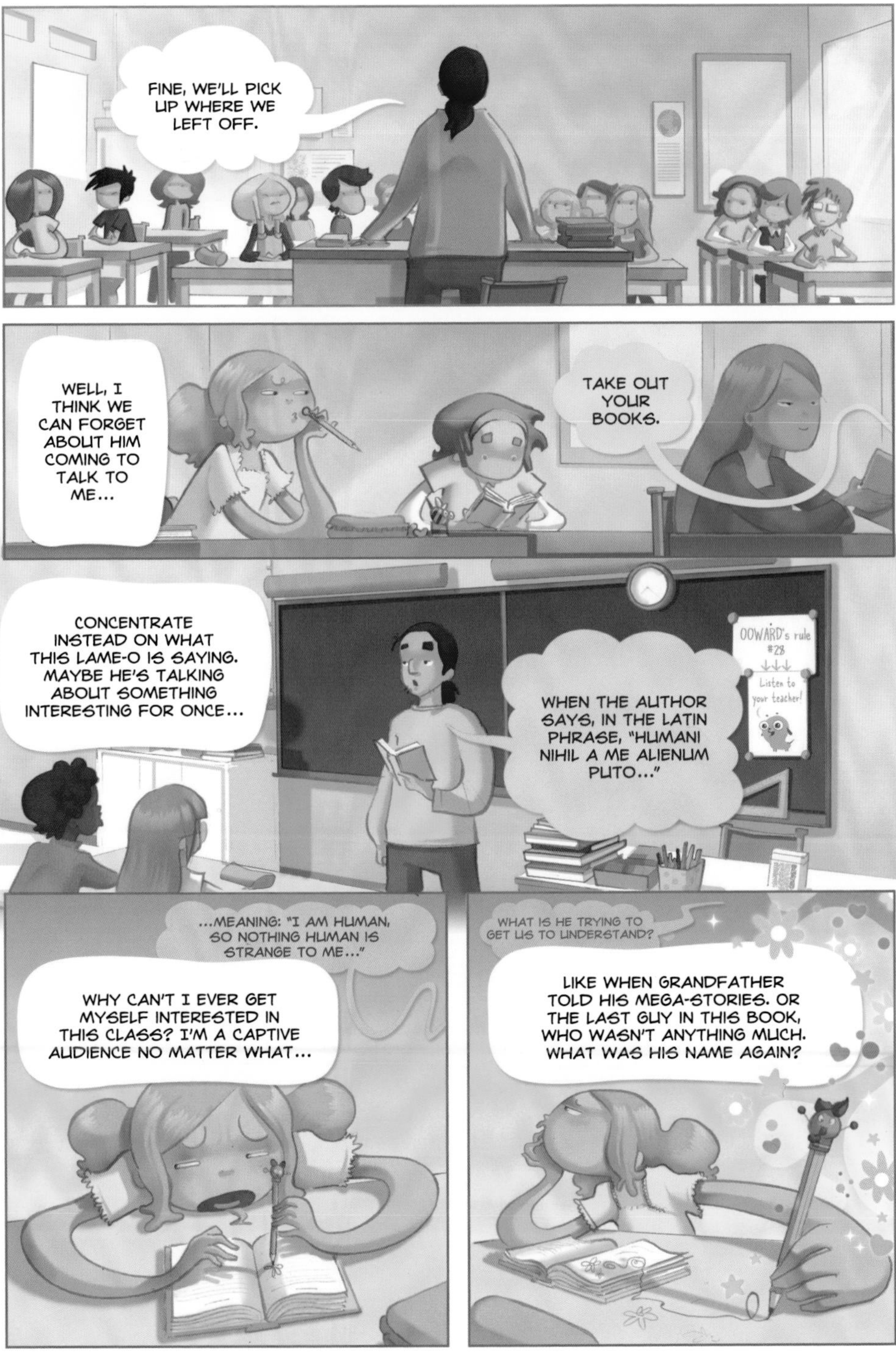
FINE, WE'LL PICK UP WHERE WE LEFT OFF.
WELL, I THINK WE CAN FORGET ABOUT HIM COMING TO TALK TO ME...
TAKE OUT YOUR BOOKS.
CONCENTRATE INSTEAD ON WHAT THIS LAME-O IS SAYING. MAYBE HE'S TALKING ABOUT SOMETHING INTERESTING FOR ONCE...
WHEN THE AUTHOR SAYS, IN THE LATIN PHRASE, "HUMANI NIHIL A ME ALIENUM PUTO..."
OOWARD's rule #28
Listen to your teacher!
...MEANING: "I AM HUMAN, SO NOTHING HUMAN IS STRANGE TO ME..."
WHY CAN'T I EVER GET MYSELF INTERESTED IN THIS CLASS? I'M A CAPTIVE AUDIENCE NO MATTER WHAT...
WHAT IS HE TRYING TO GET US TO UNDERSTAND?
LIKE WHEN GRANDFATHER TOLD HIS MEGA-STORIES. OR THE LAST GUY IN THIS BOOK, WHO WASN'T ANYTHING MUCH. WHAT WAS HIS NAME AGAIN?

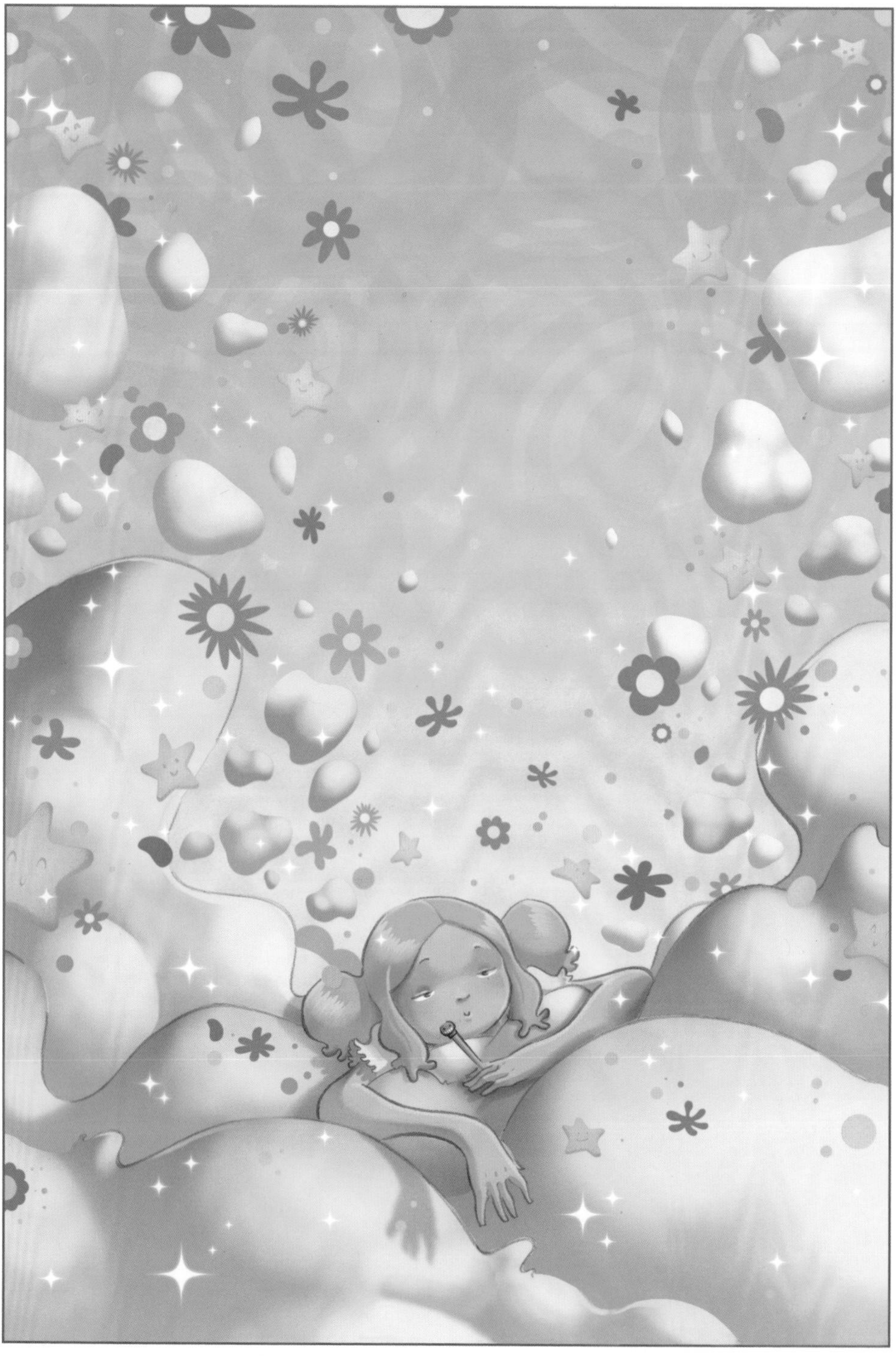

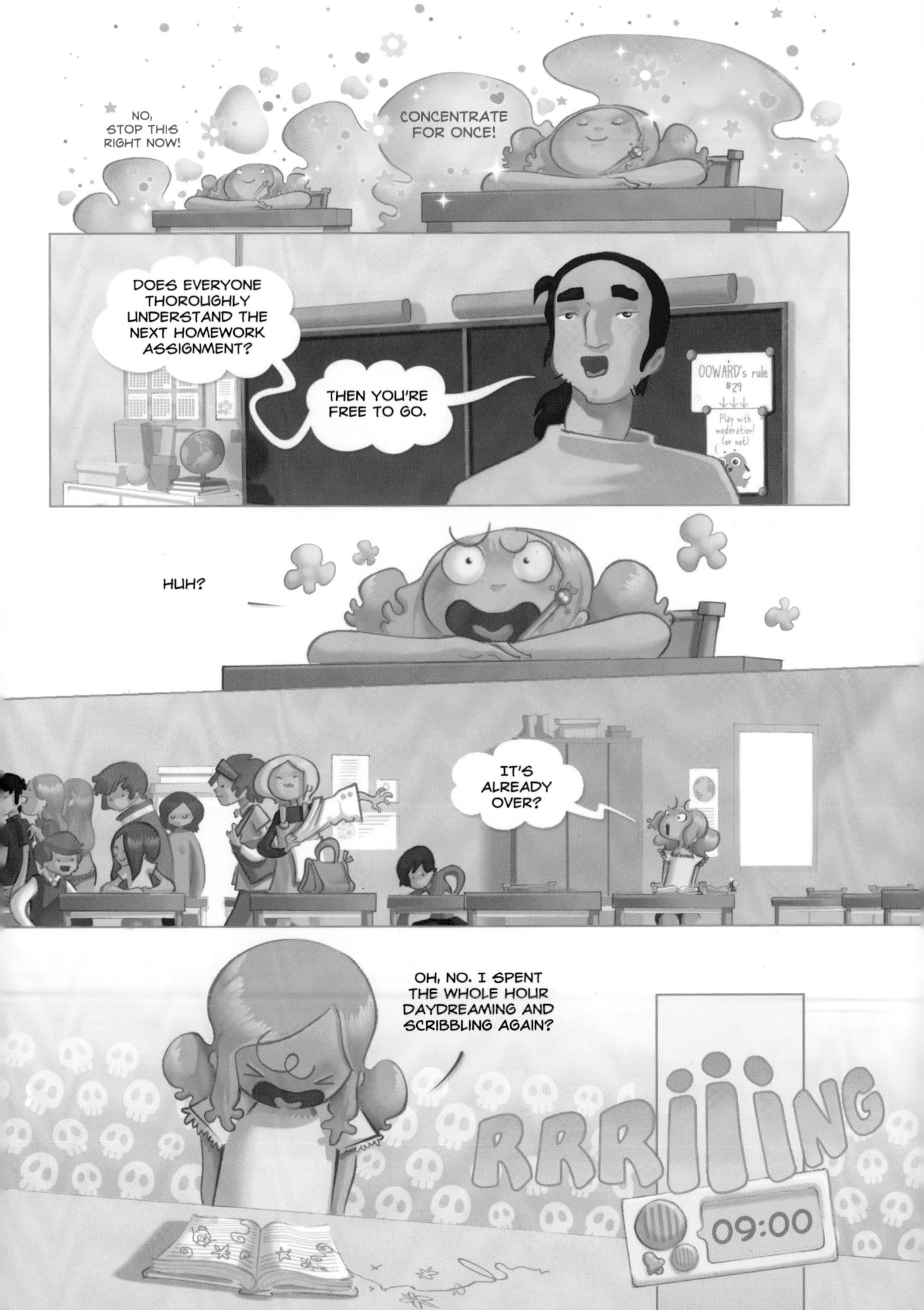
NO, STOP THIS RIGHT NOW!
CONCENTRATE FOR ONCE!
DOES EVERYONE THOROUGHLY UNDERSTAND THE NEXT HOMEWORK ASSIGNMENT?
THEN YOU'RE FREE TO GO.
OOWARD's rule #29
Play with moderation! (or not)
HUH?
IT'S ALREADY OVER?
OH, NO. I SPENT THE WHOLE HOUR DAYDREAMING AND SCRIBBLING AGAIN?
RRRIIING
09:00

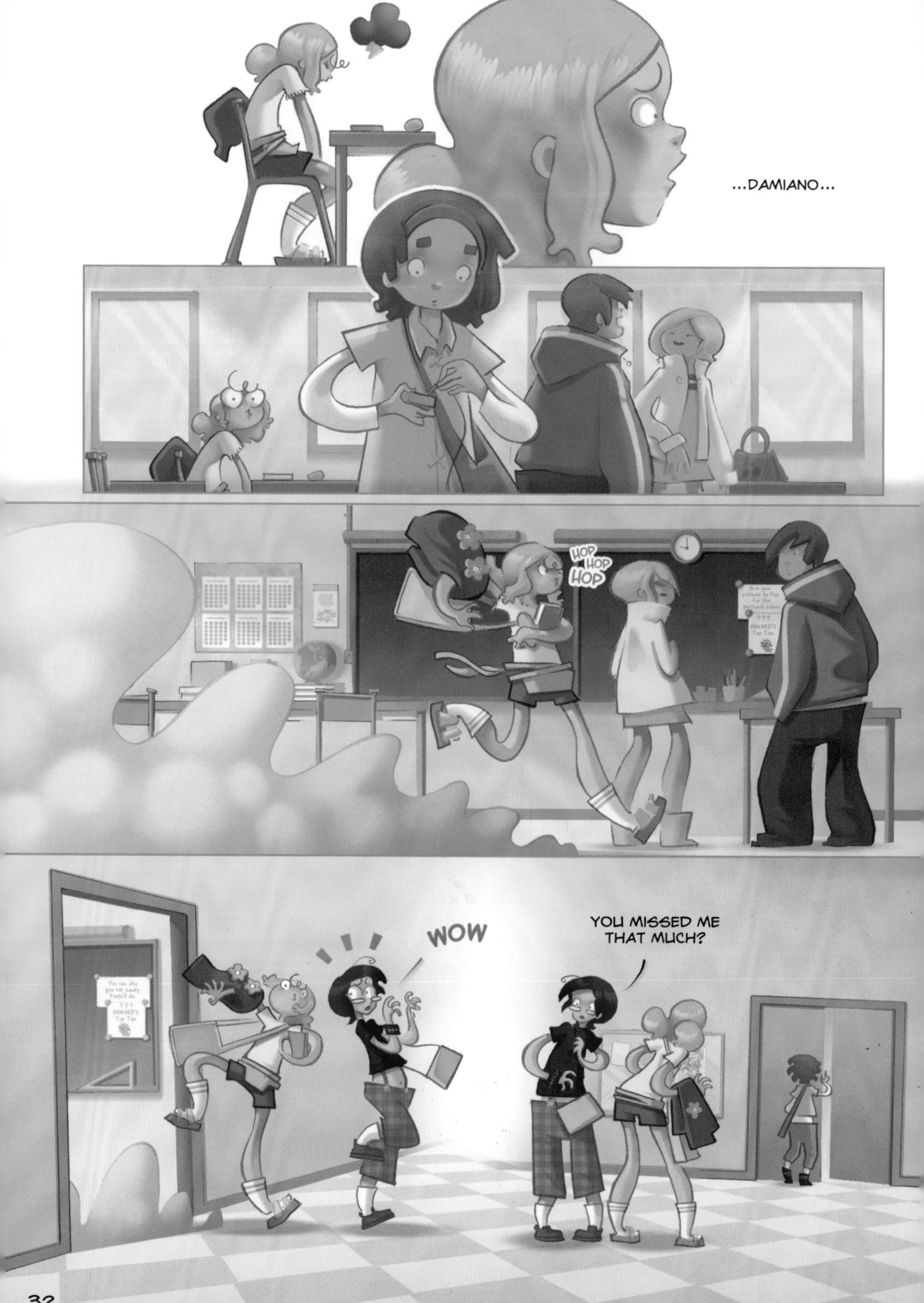
...DAMIANO...
HOP HOP HOP
WOW
YOU MISSED ME THAT MUCH?

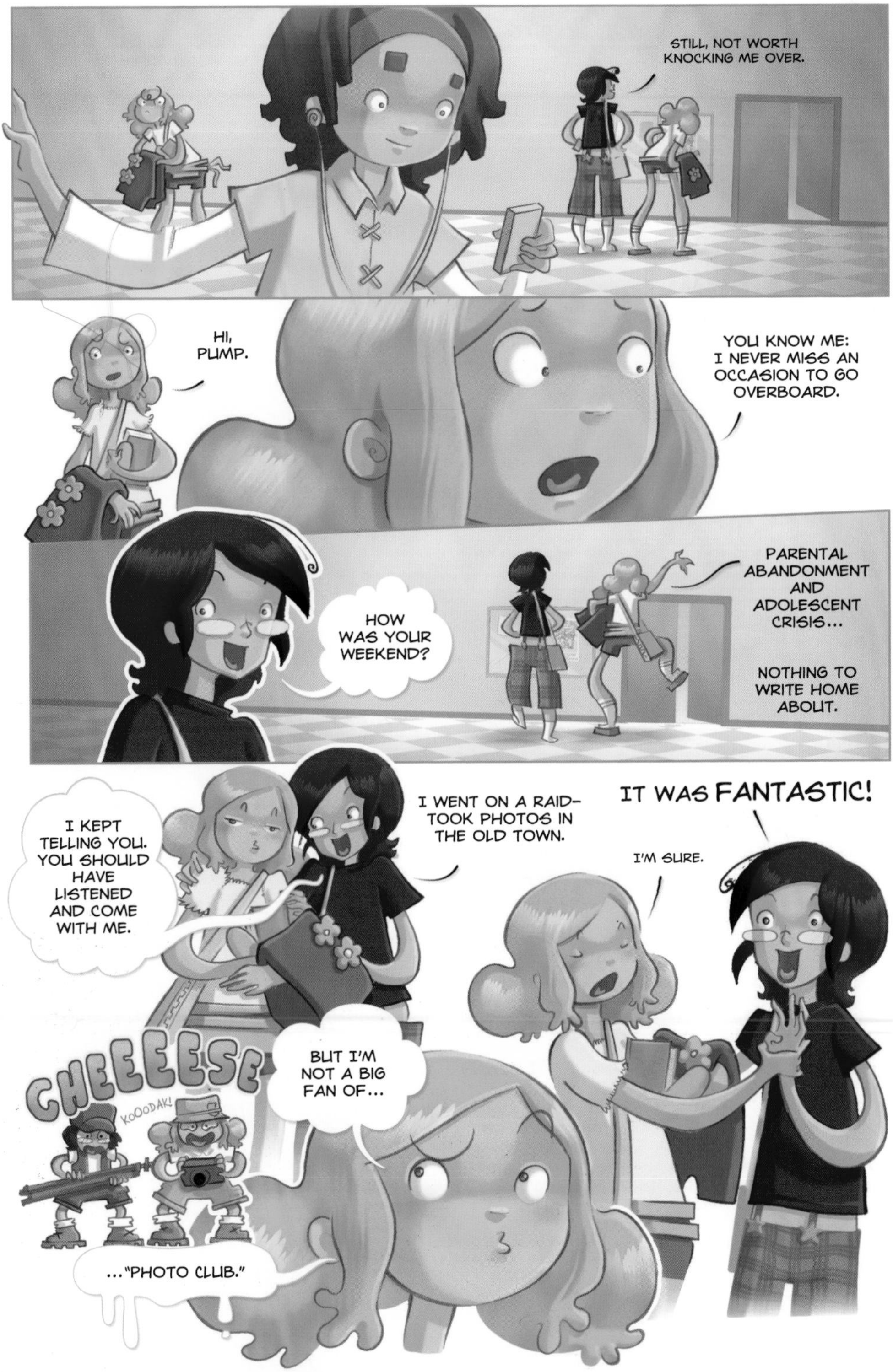
STILL, NOT WORTH KNOCKING ME OVER.
HI, PUMP.
YOU KNOW ME: I NEVER MISS AN OCCASION TO GO OVERBOARD.
HOW WAS YOUR WEEKEND?
PARENTAL ABANDONMENT AND ADOLESCENT CRISIS...
NOTHING TO WRITE HOME ABOUT.
IT WAS FANTASTIC!
I'M SURE.
I WENT ON A RAID-TOOK PHOTOS IN THE OLD TOWN.
I KEPT TELLING YOU. YOU SHOULD HAVE LISTENED AND COME WITH ME.
BUT I'M NOT A BIG FAN OF...
CHEEEESE
KOOODAK!
..."PHOTO CLUB."

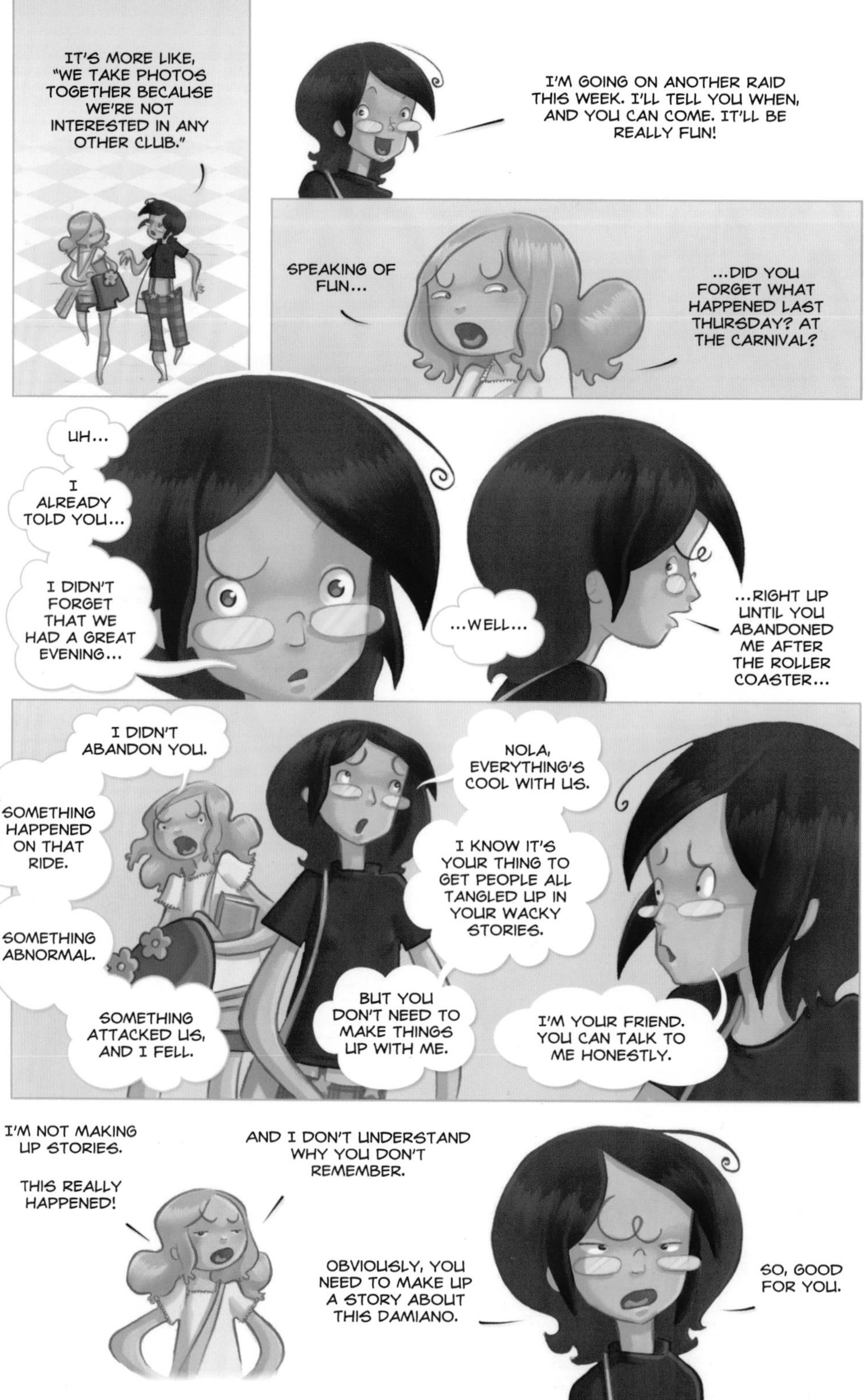
IT'S MORE LIKE, "WE TAKE PHOTOS TOGETHER BECAUSE WE'RE NOT INTERESTED IN ANY OTHER CLUB."
I'M GOING ON ANOTHER RAID THIS WEEK. I'LL TELL YOU WHEN, AND YOU CAN COME. IT'LL BE REALLY FUN!
SPEAKING OF FUN...
...DID YOU FORGET WHAT HAPPENED LAST THURSDAY? AT THE CARNIVAL?
UH...
I ALREADY TOLD YOU...
I DIDN'T FORGET THAT WE HAD A GREAT EVENING...
...WELL...
...RIGHT UP UNTIL YOU ABANDONED ME AFTER THE ROLLER COASTER...
I DIDN'T ABANDON YOU.
SOMETHING HAPPENED ON THAT RIDE.
SOMETHING ABNORMAL.
SOMETHING ATTACKED US, AND I FELL.
NOLA, EVERYTHING'S COOL WITH US.
I KNOW IT'S YOUR THING TO GET PEOPLE ALL TANGLED UP IN YOUR WACKY STORIES.
BUT YOU DON'T NEED TO MAKE THINGS UP WITH ME.
I'M YOUR FRIEND. YOU CAN TALK TO ME HONESTLY.
I'M NOT MAKING UP STORIES.
THIS REALLY HAPPENED!
AND I DON'T UNDERSTAND WHY YOU DON'T REMEMBER.
OBVIOUSLY, YOU NEED TO MAKE UP A STORY ABOUT THIS DAMIANO.
SO, GOOD FOR YOU.

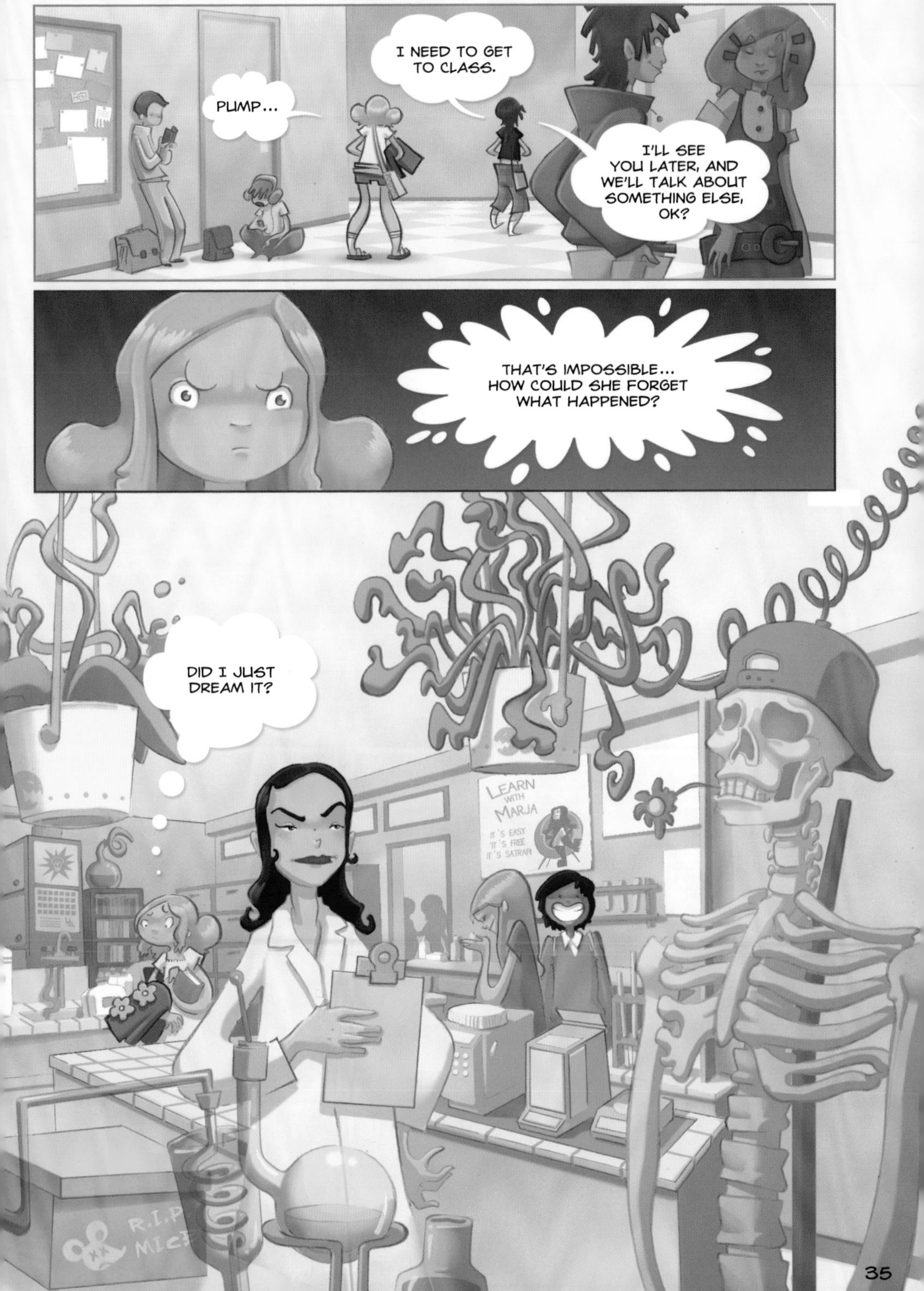
PUMP...
I NEED TO GET TO CLASS.
I'LL SEE YOU LATER, AND WE'LL TALK ABOUT SOMETHING ELSE, OK?
THAT'S IMPOSSIBLE... HOW COULD SHE FORGET WHAT HAPPENED?
DID I JUST DREAM IT?
LEARN WITH MARJA
IT'S EASY
IT'S FREE
IT'S SATRAPI

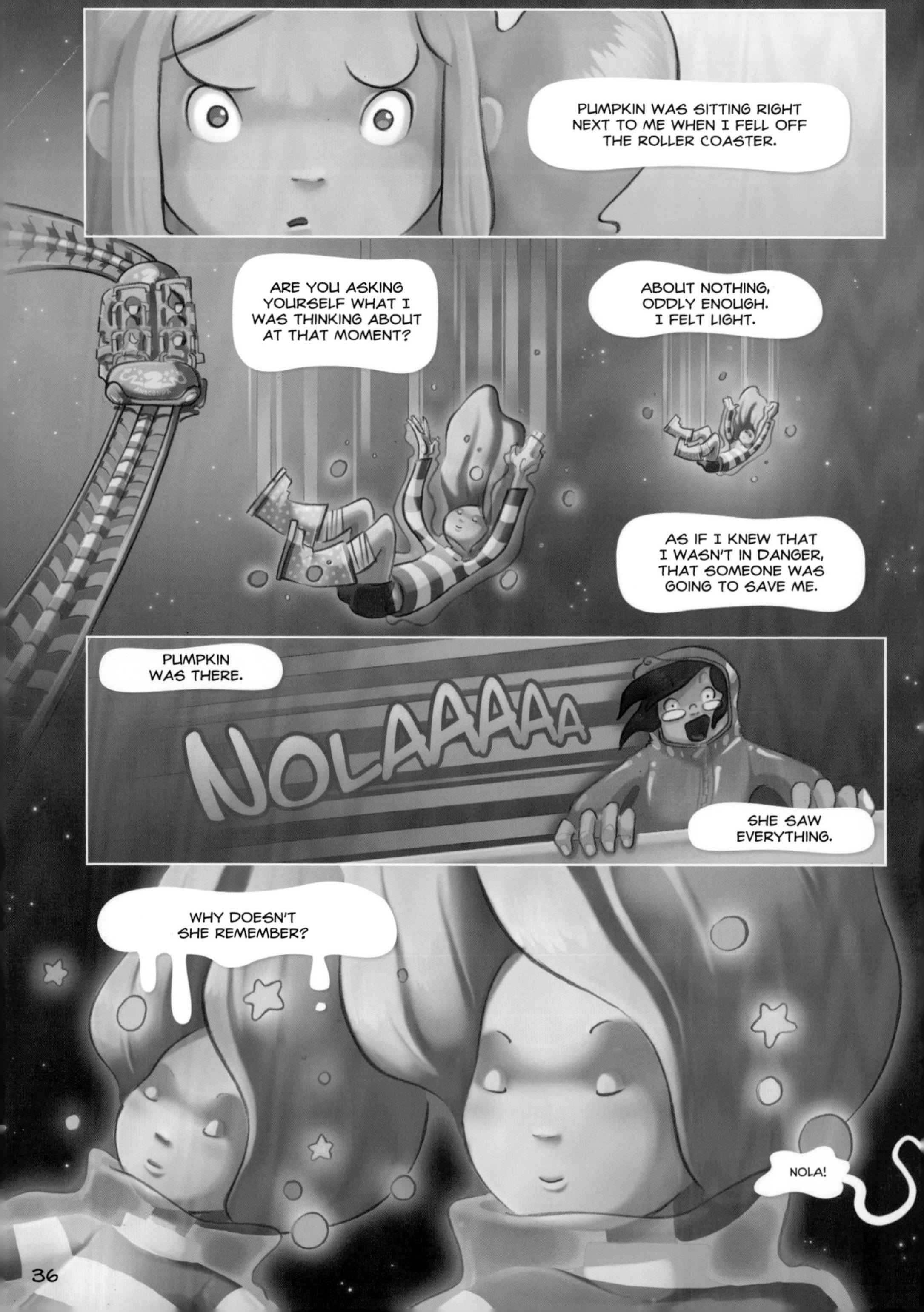
PUMPKIN WAS SITTING RIGHT NEXT TO ME WHEN I FELL OFF THE ROLLER COASTER.
ARE YOU ASKING YOURSELF WHAT I WAS THINKING ABOUT AT THAT MOMENT?
ABOUT NOTHING, ODDLY ENOUGH. I FELT LIGHT.
AS IF I KNEW THAT I WASN'T IN DANGER, THAT SOMEONE WAS GOING TO SAVE ME.
PUMPKIN WAS THERE.
NOLAAAAA
SHE SAW EVERYTHING.
WHY DOESN'T SHE REMEMBER?
NOLA!

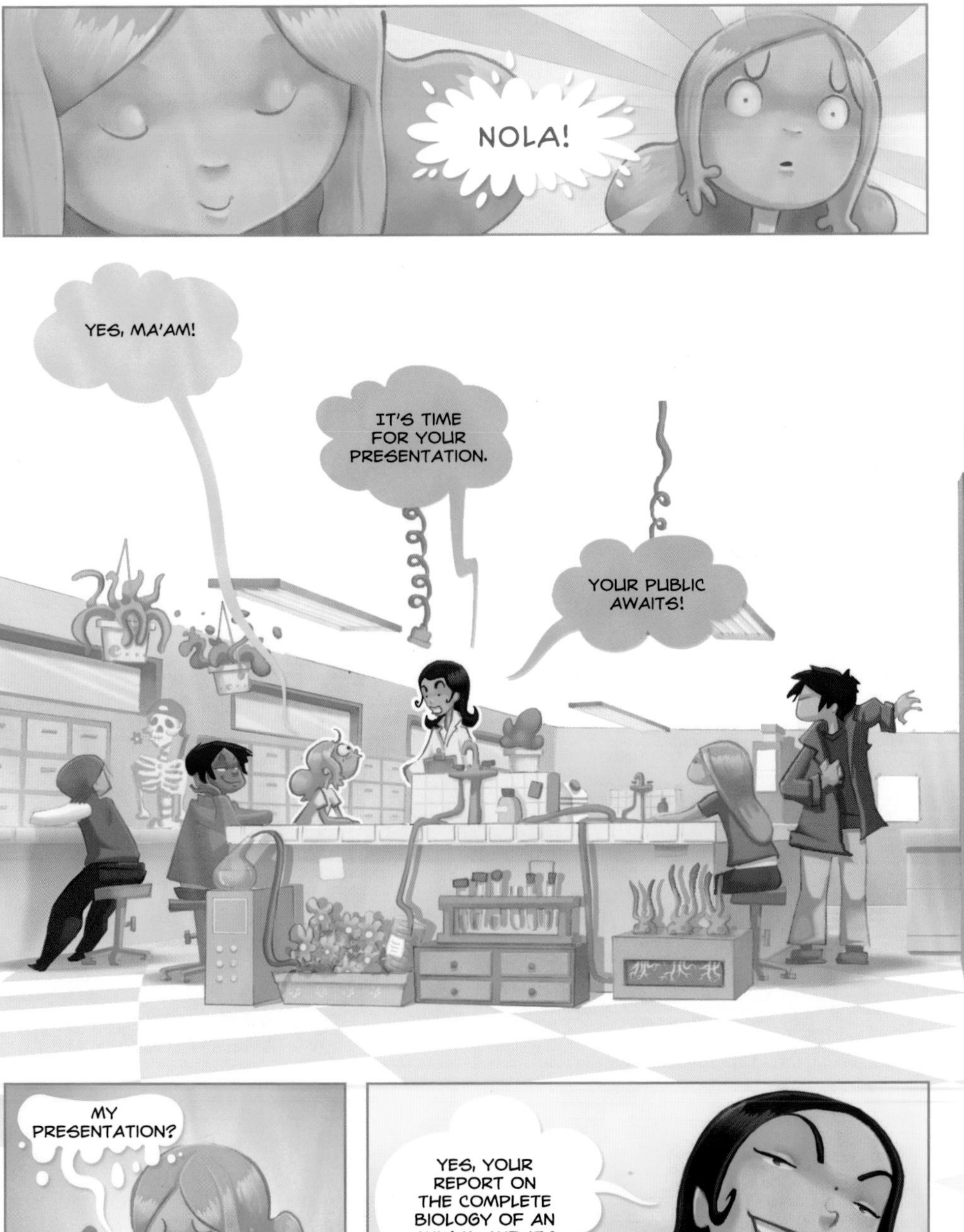
NOLA!
YES, MA'AM!
IT'S TIME FOR YOUR PRESENTATION.
YOUR PUBLIC AWAITS!
MY PRESENTATION?
YES, YOUR REPORT ON THE COMPLETE BIOLOGY OF AN ANIMAL AND ITS VARIOUS VITAL FUNCTIONS.

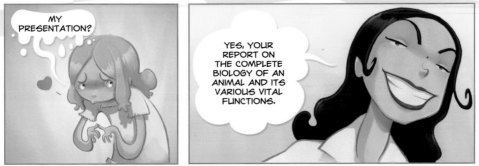

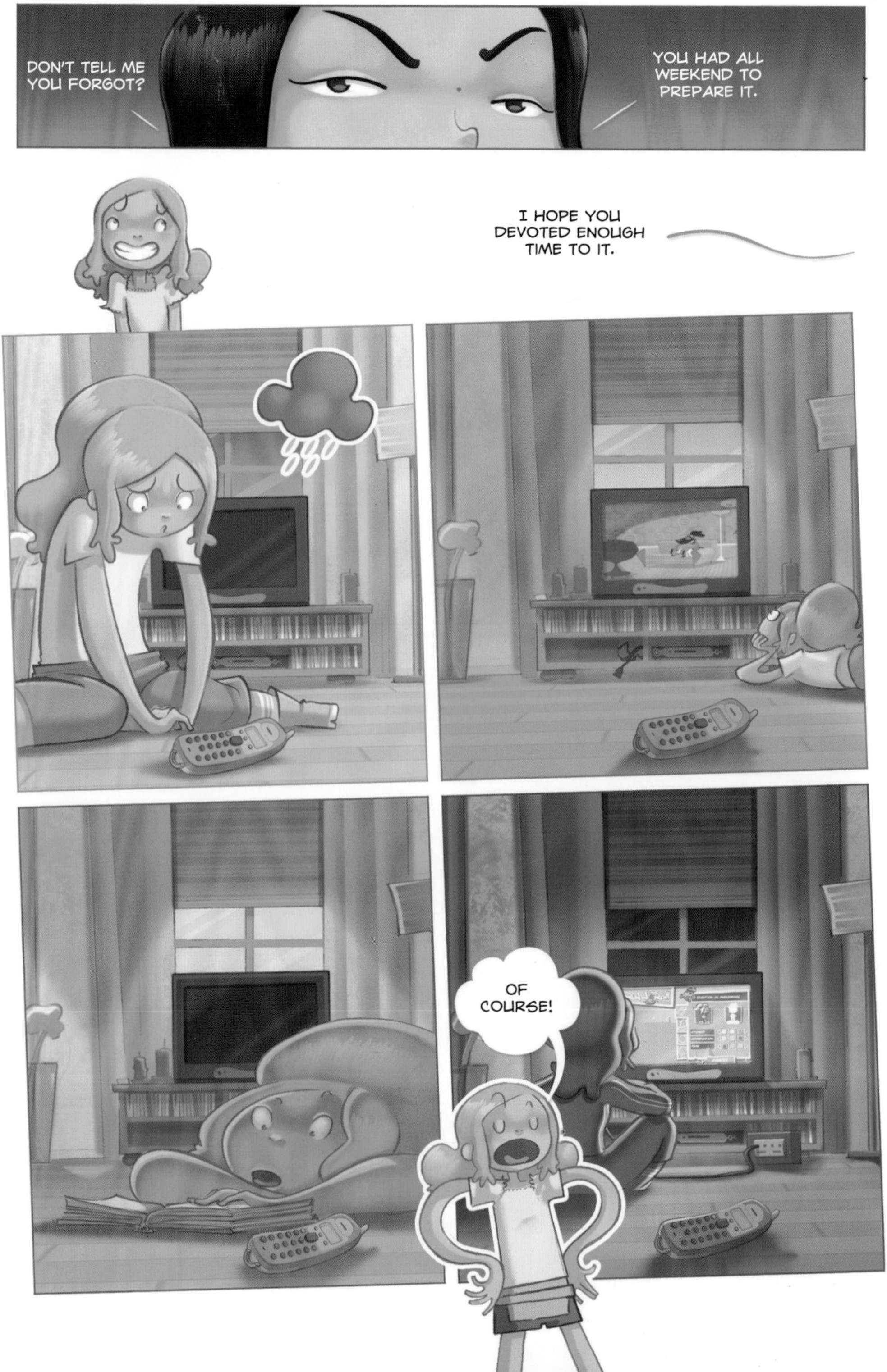
DON'T TELL ME YOU FORGOT?
YOU HAD ALL WEEKEND TO PREPARE IT.
I HOPE YOU DEVOTED ENOUGH TIME TO IT.
OF COURSE!

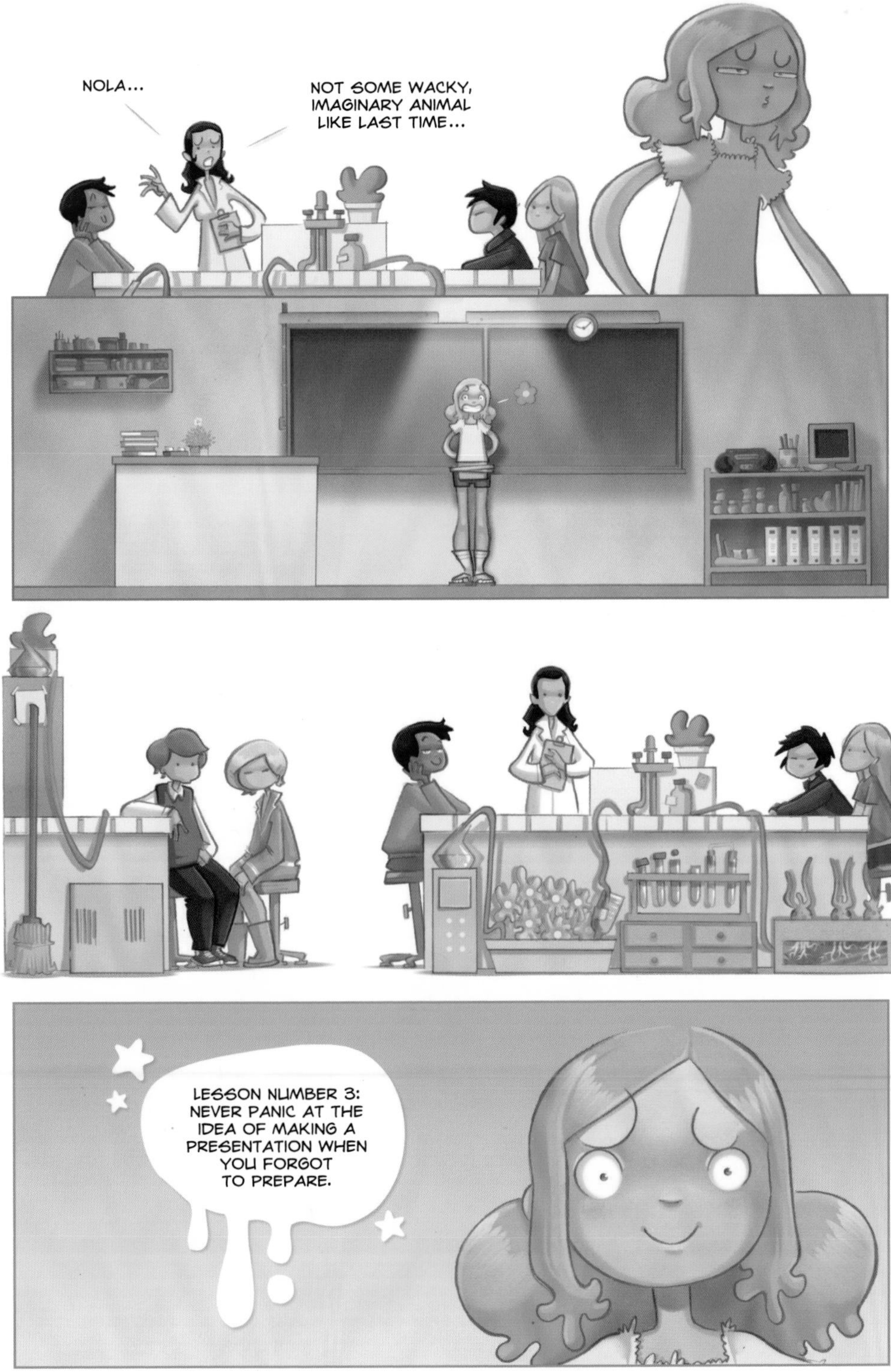
NOLA...
NOT SOME WACKY, IMAGINARY ANIMAL LIKE LAST TIME...
LESSON NUMBER 3: NEVER PANIC AT THE IDEA OF MAKING A PRESENTATION WHEN YOU FORGOT TO PREPARE.

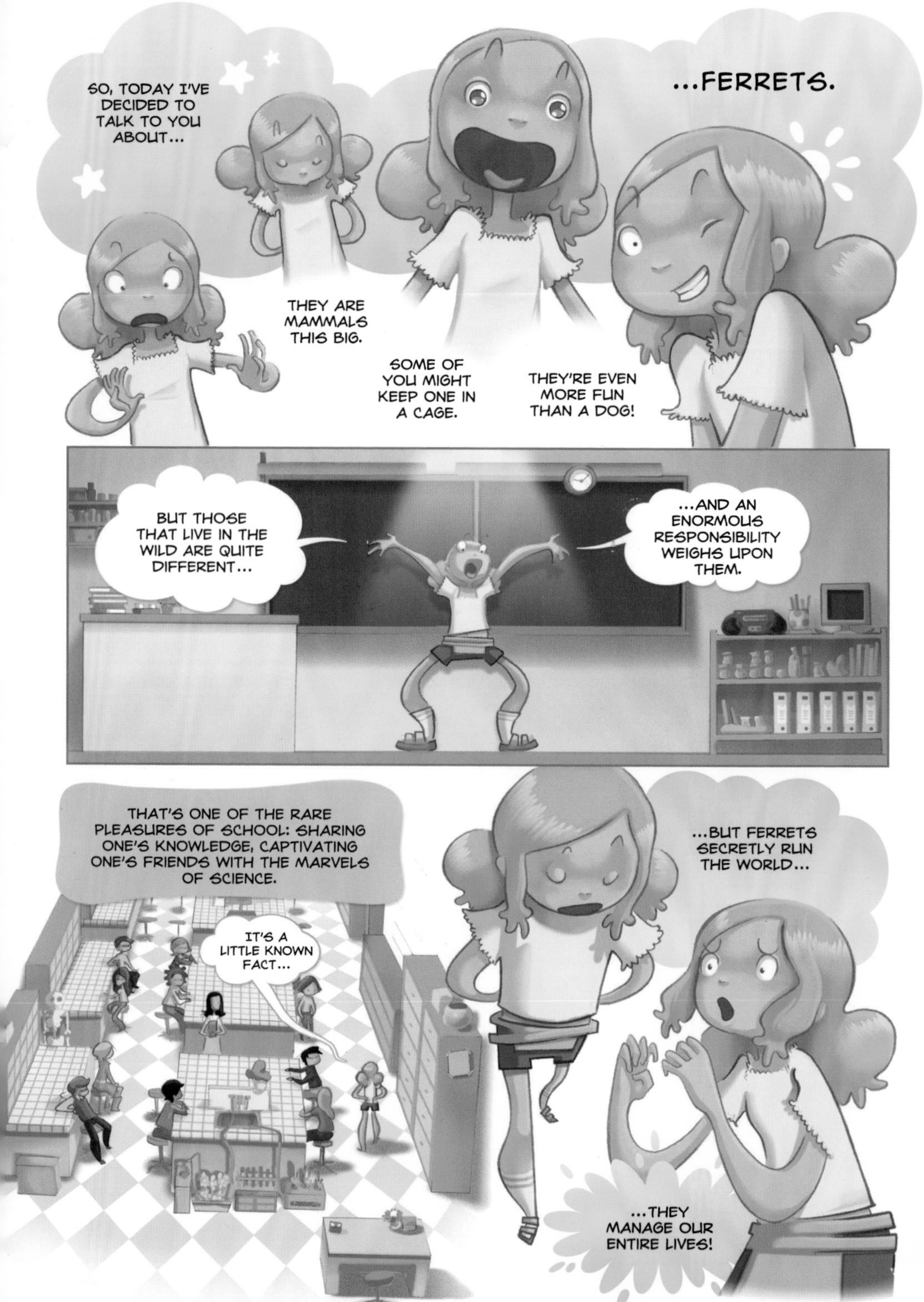
SO, TODAY I'VE DECIDED TO TALK TO YOU ABOUT...
...FERRETS.
THEY ARE MAMMALS THIS BIG.
SOME OF YOU MIGHT KEEP ONE IN A CAGE.
THEY'RE EVEN MORE FUN THAN A DOG!
BUT THOSE THAT LIVE IN THE WILD ARE QUITE DIFFERENT...
...AND AN ENORMOUS RESPONSIBILITY WEIGHS UPON THEM.
THAT'S ONE OF THE RARE PLEASURES OF SCHOOL: SHARING ONE'S KNOWLEDGE, CAPTIVATING ONE'S FRIENDS WITH THE MARVELS OF SCIENCE.
IT'S A LITTLE KNOWN FACT...
...BUT FERRETS SECRETLY RUN THE WORLD...
...THEY MANAGE OUR ENTIRE LIVES!

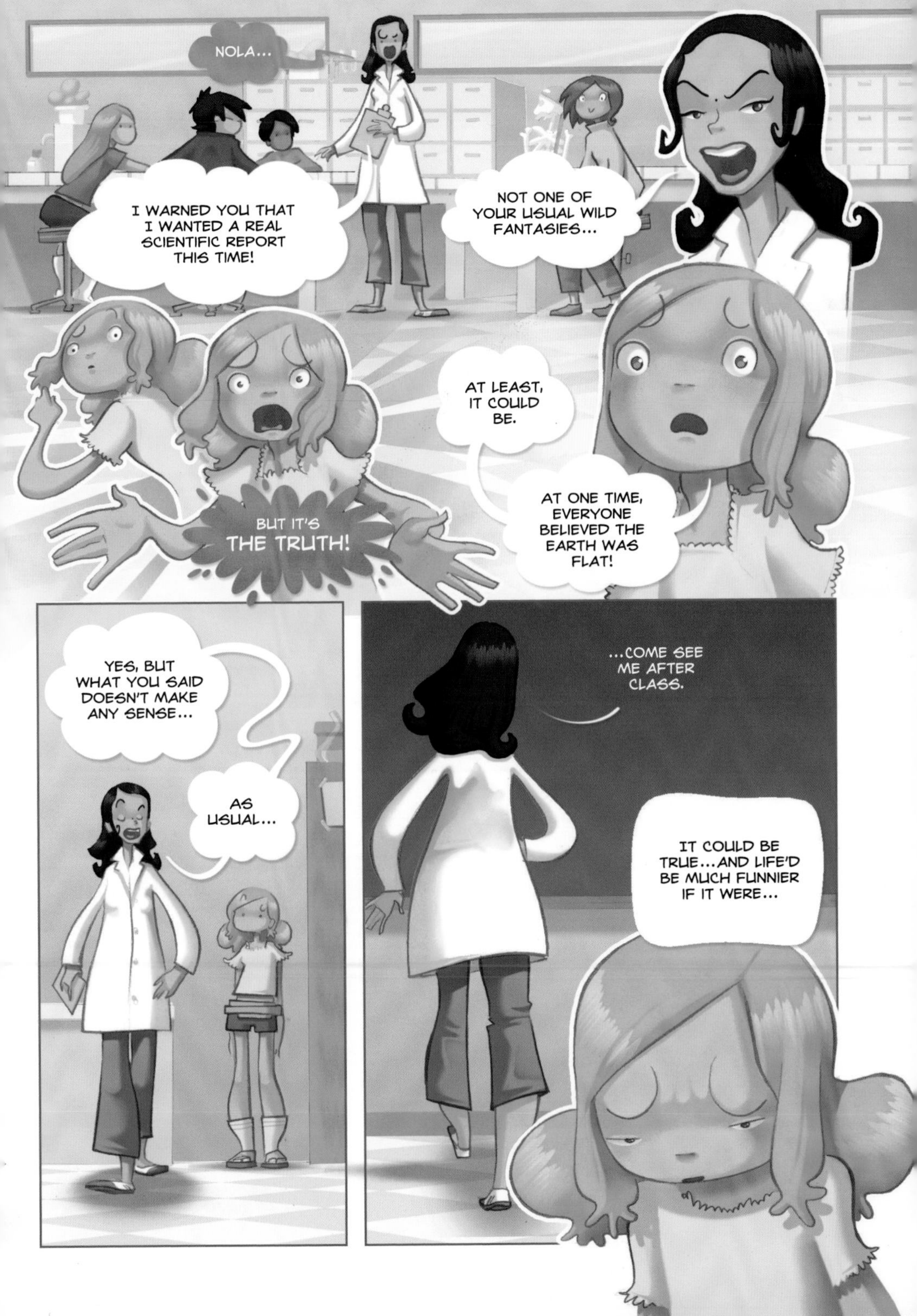
NOLA...
I WARNED YOU THAT I WANTED A REAL SCIENTIFIC REPORT THIS TIME!
NOT ONE OF YOUR USUAL WILD FANTASIES...
BUT IT'S THE TRUTH!
AT LEAST, IT COULD BE.
AT ONE TIME, EVERYONE BELIEVED THE EARTH WAS FLAT!
YES, BUT WHAT YOU SAID DOESN'T MAKE ANY SENSE...
AS USUAL...
...COME SEE ME AFTER CLASS.
IT COULD BE TRUE...AND LIFE'D BE MUCH FUNNIER IF IT WERE...

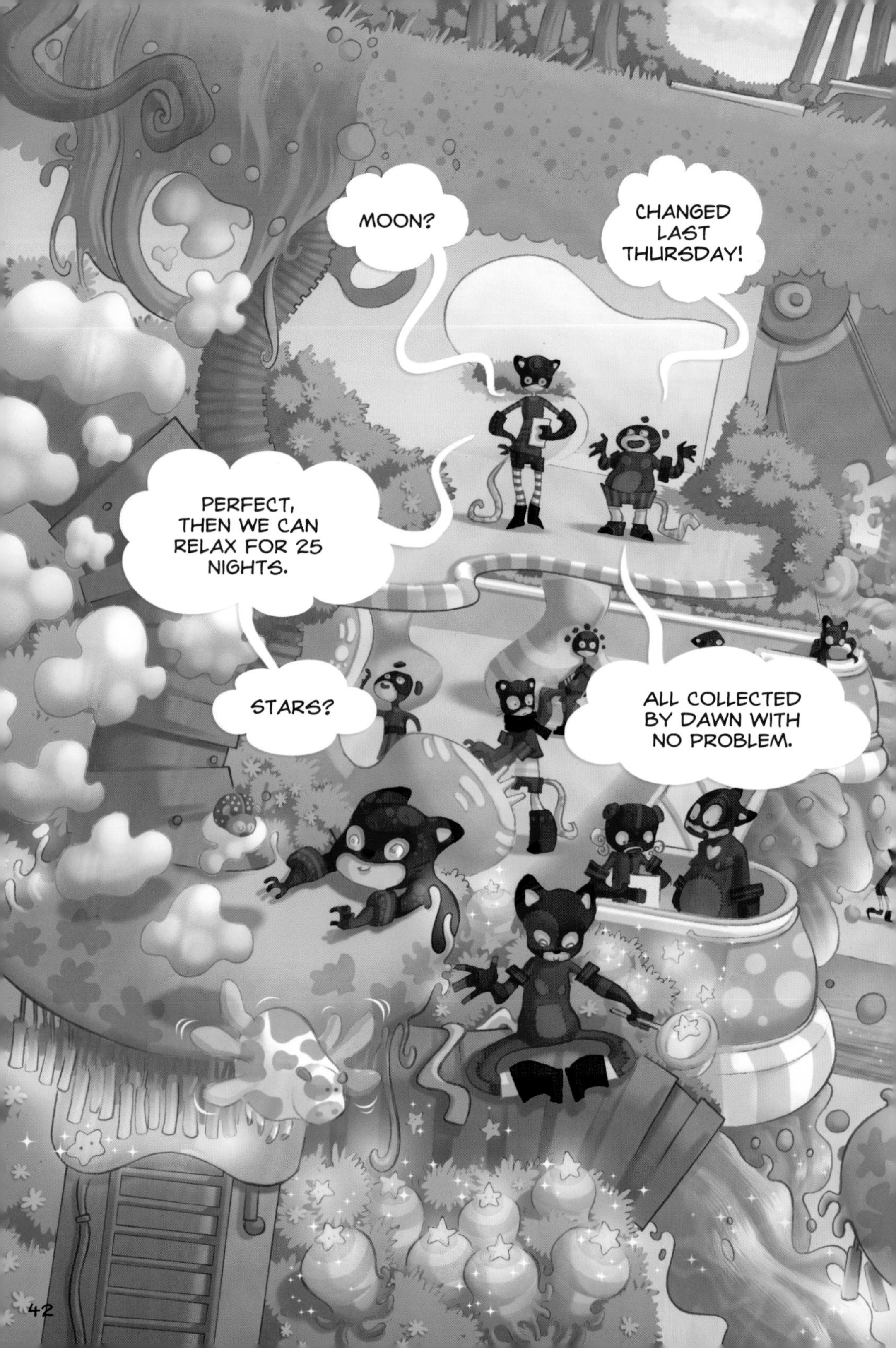
MOON?
CHANGED LAST THURSDAY!
PERFECT, THEN WE CAN RELAX FOR 25 NIGHTS.
STARS?
ALL COLLECTED BY DAWN WITH NO PROBLEM.

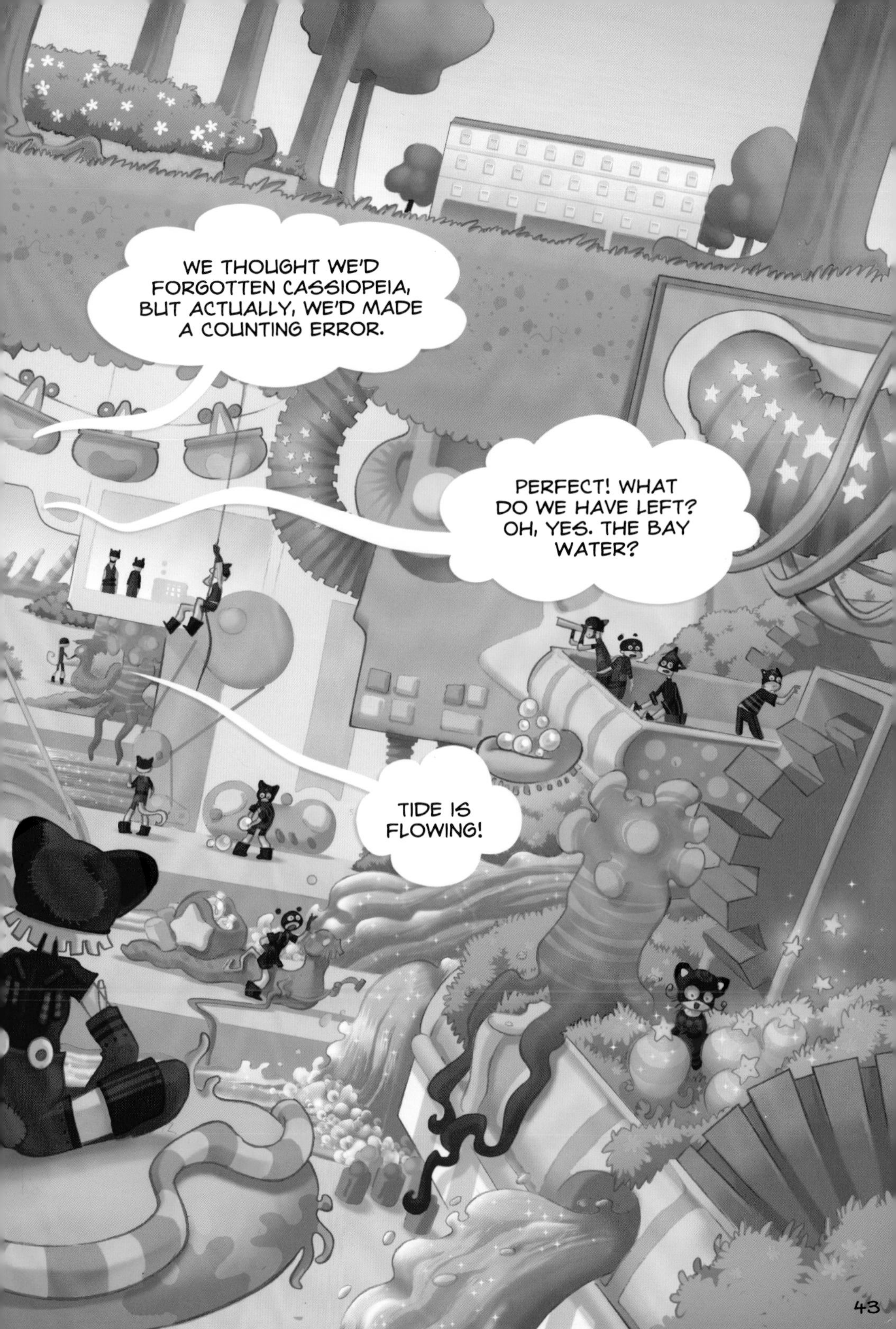
WE THOUGHT WE'D FORGOTTEN CASSIOPEIA, BUT ACTUALLY, WE'D MADE A COUNTING ERROR.
PERFECT! WHAT DO WE HAVE LEFT? OH, YES. THE BAY WATER?
TIDE IS FLOWING!

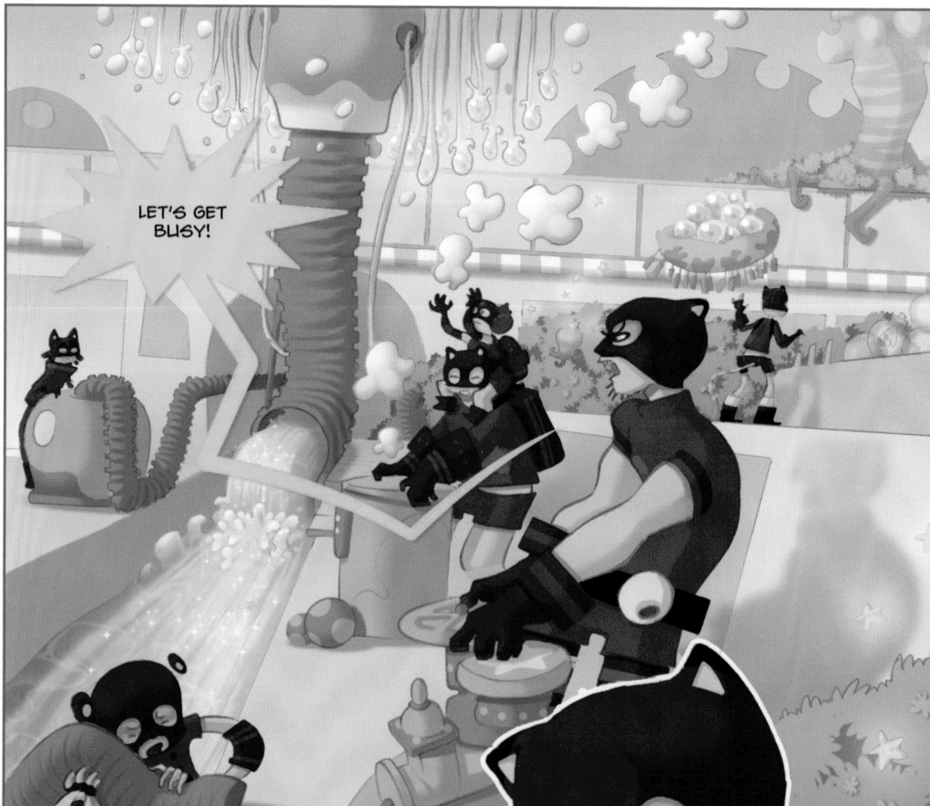
LET'S GET BUSY!
AFTER THE WEEKEND, THE WATER IS ALWAYS FILTHY!

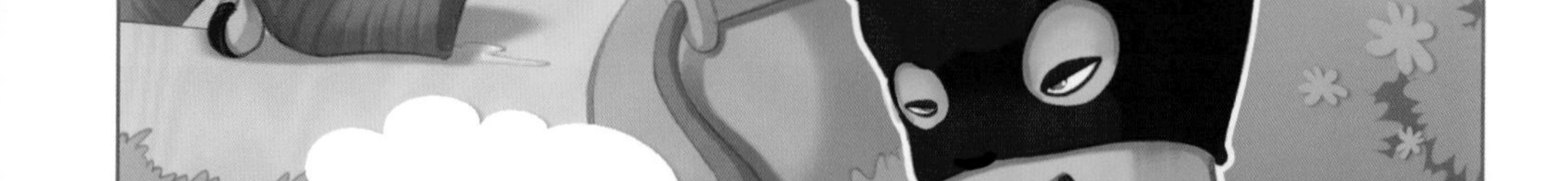
WSSHH

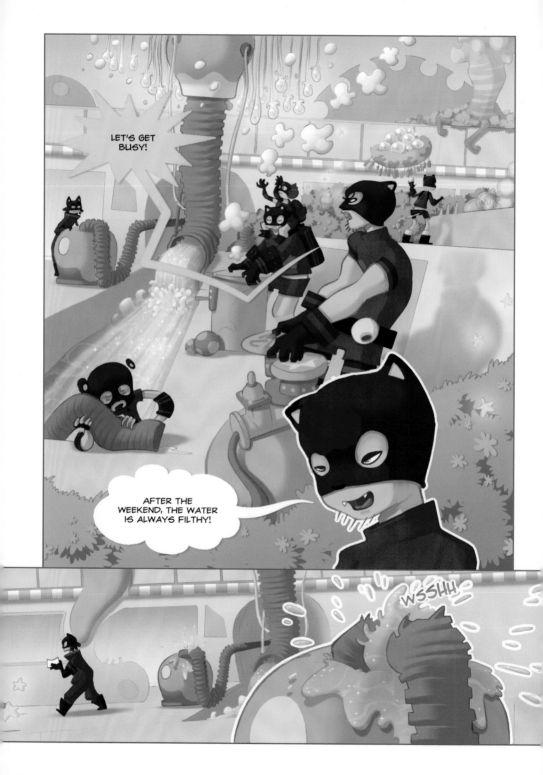

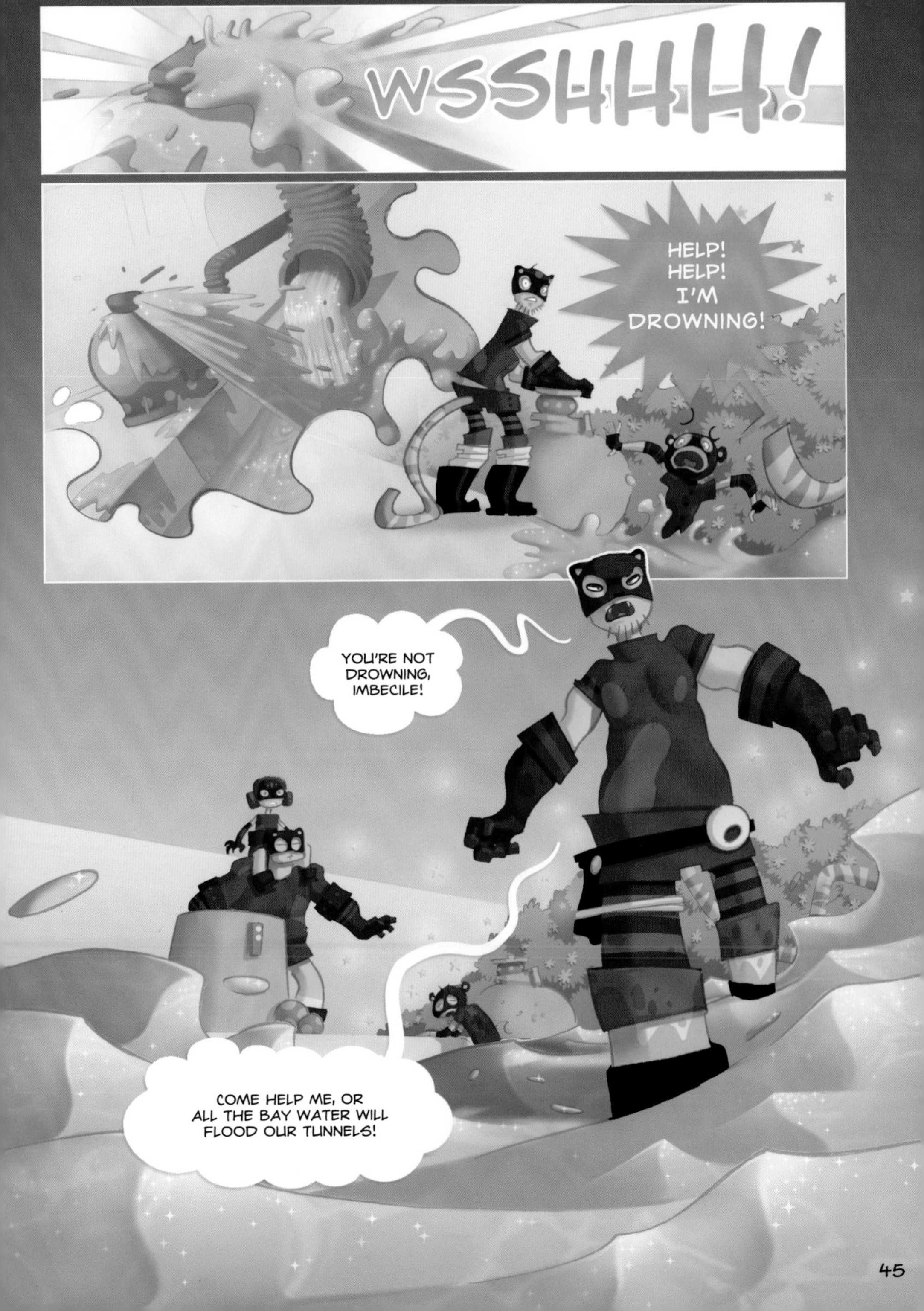
WSSHHH!
HELP! HELP! I'M DROWNING!
YOU'RE NOT DROWNING, IMBECILE!
COME HELP ME, OR ALL THE BAY WATER WILL FLOOD OUR TUNNELS!

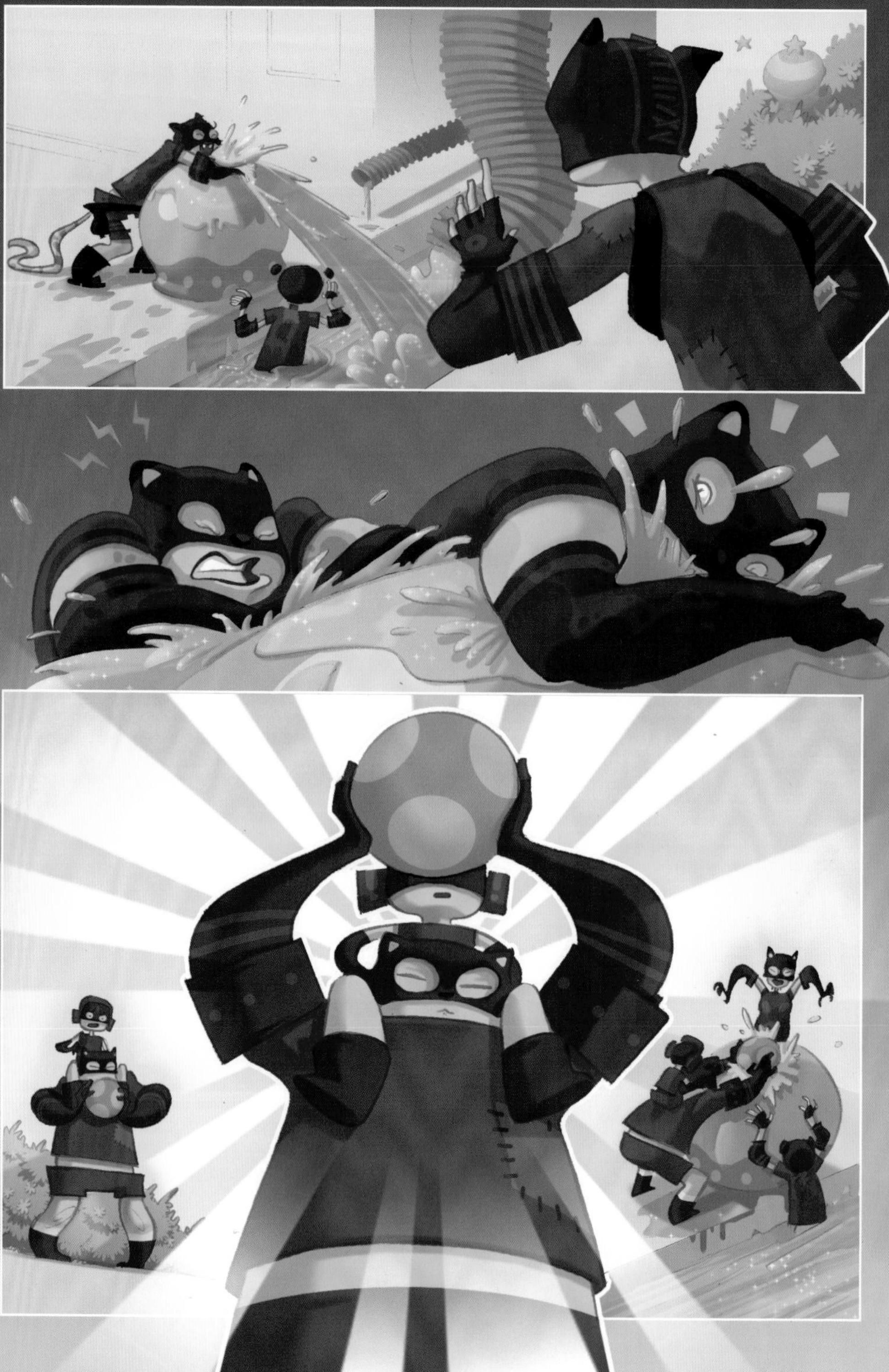

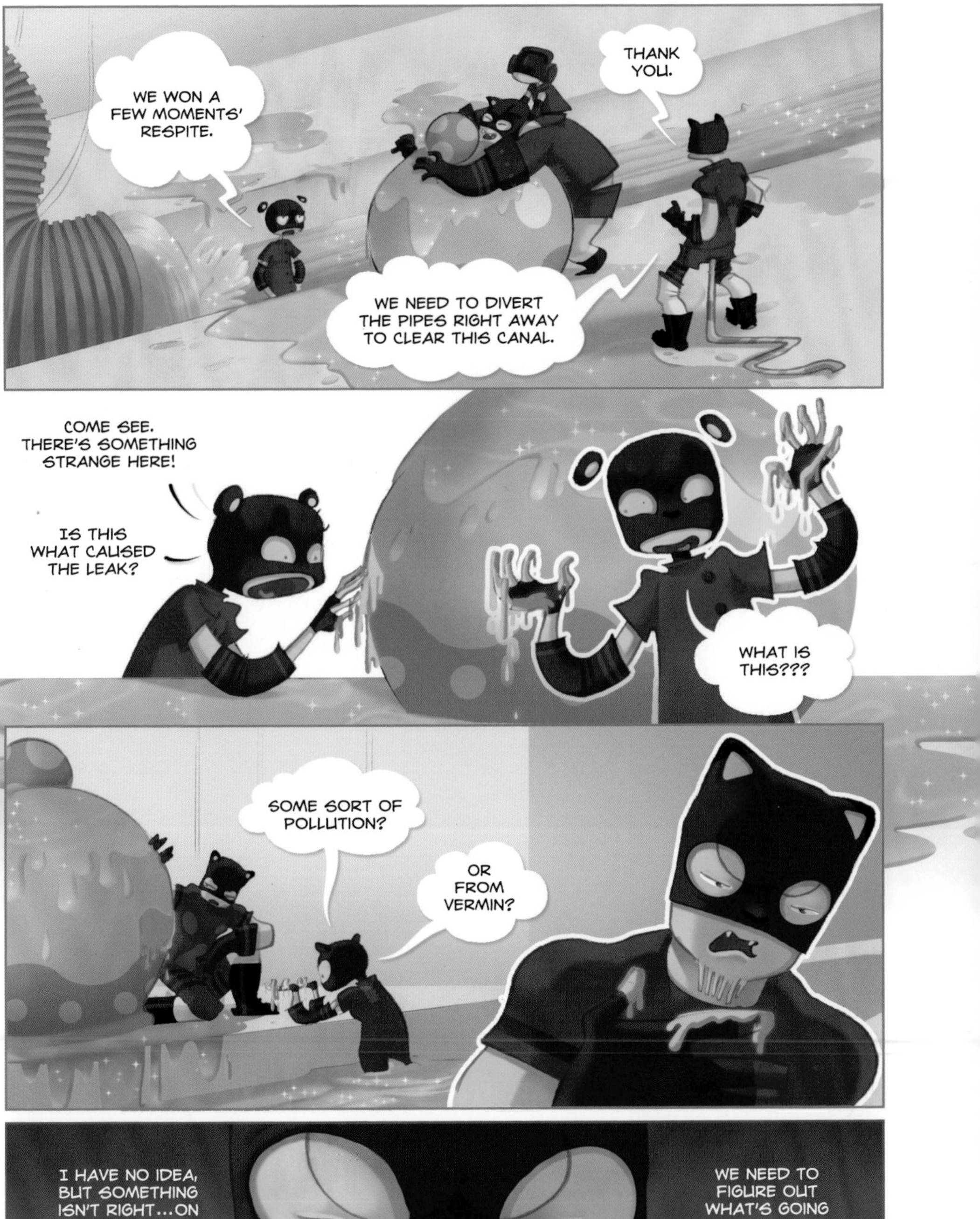
WE WON A FEW MOMENTS' RESPITE.
THANK YOU.
WE NEED TO DIVERT THE PIPES RIGHT AWAY TO CLEAR THIS CANAL.
COME SEE. THERE'S SOMETHING STRANGE HERE!
IS THIS WHAT CAUSED THE LEAK?
WHAT IS THIS???
SOME SORT OF POLLUTION?
OR FROM VERMIN?
I HAVE NO IDEA, BUT SOMETHING ISN'T RIGHT...ON ONE SIDE OR THE OTHER OF THIS WORLD...
WE NEED TO FIGURE OUT WHAT'S GOING ON RIGHT AWAY. OR WE WILL LOSE CONTROL OF THIS TOWN.

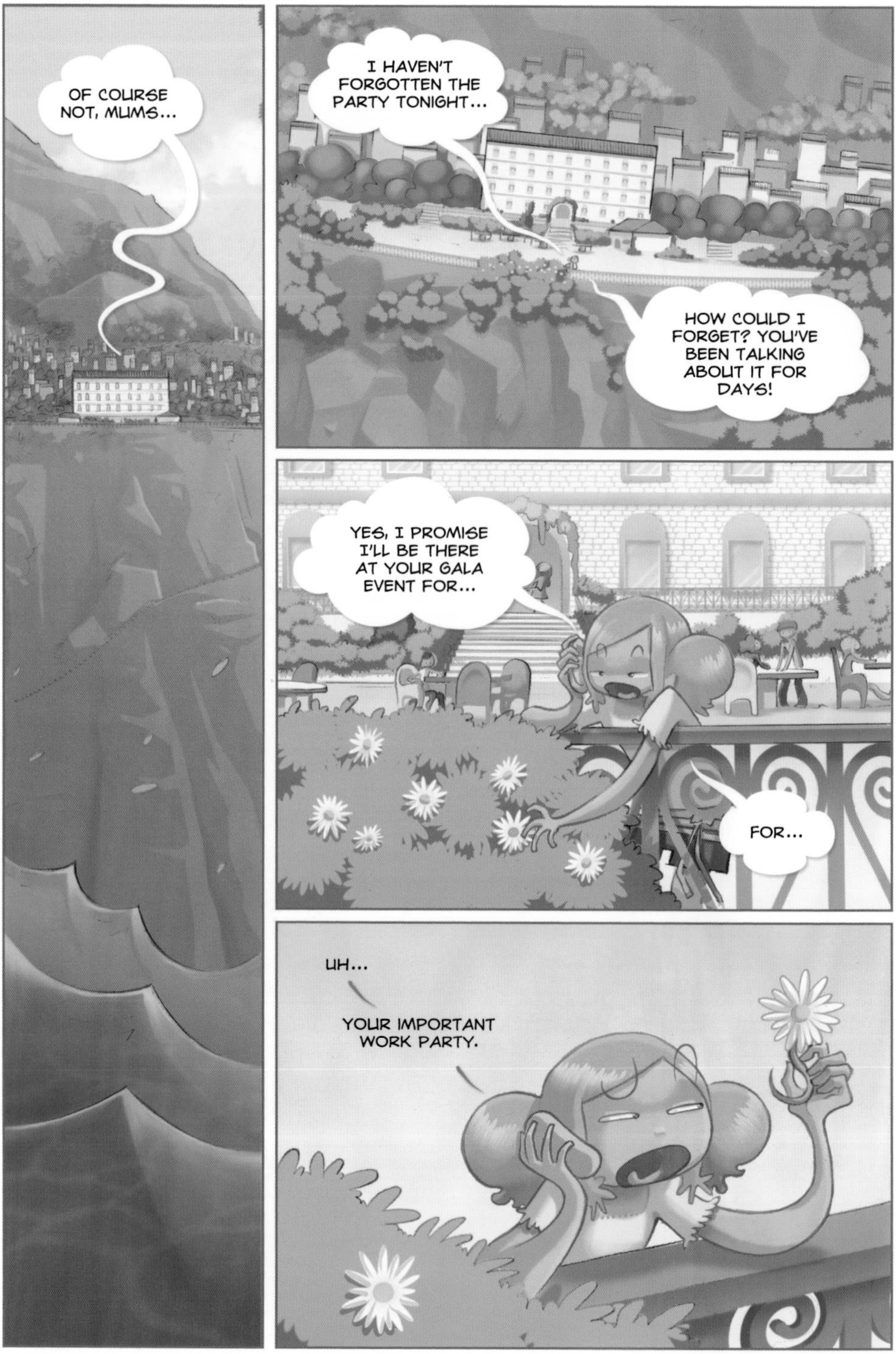
OF COURSE NOT, MUMS...
I HAVEN'T FORGOTTEN THE PARTY TONIGHT...
HOW COULD I FORGET? YOU'VE BEEN TALKING ABOUT IT FOR DAYS!
YES, I PROMISE I'LL BE THERE AT YOUR GALA EVENT FOR...
FOR...
UH...
YOUR IMPORTANT WORK PARTY.

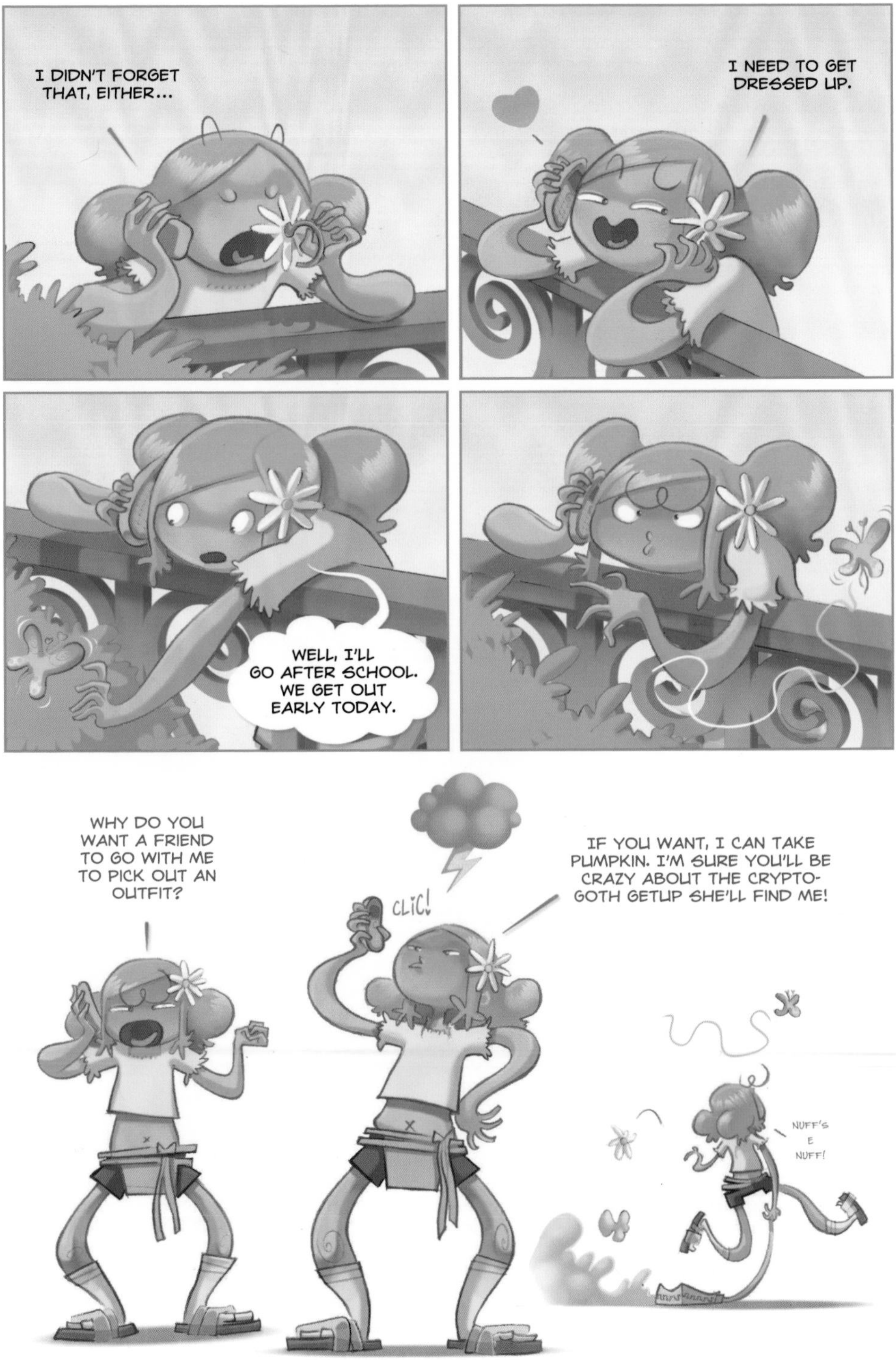
I DIDN'T FORGET THAT, EITHER...
I NEED TO GET DRESSED UP.
WELL, I'LL GO AFTER SCHOOL. WE GET OUT EARLY TODAY.
WHY DO YOU WANT A FRIEND TO GO WITH ME TO PICK OUT AN OUTFIT?
CLIC!
IF YOU WANT, I CAN TAKE PUMPKIN. I'M SURE YOU'LL BE CRAZY ABOUT THE CRYPTO-GOTH GETUP SHE'LL FIND ME!
NUFF'S E NUFF!

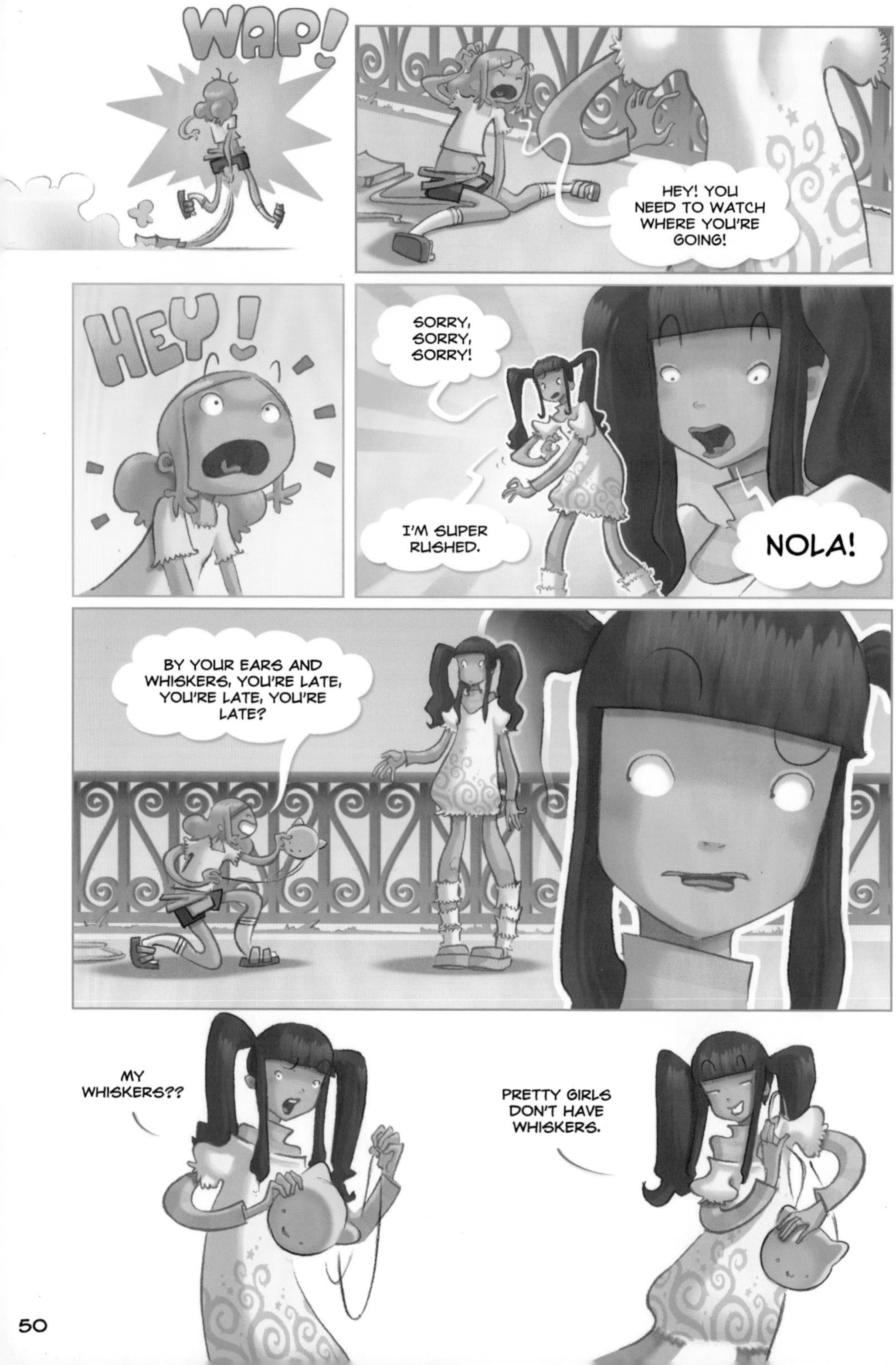
WAP!
HEY! YOU NEED TO WATCH WHERE YOU'RE GOING!
HEY!
SORRY, SORRY, SORRY!
I'M SUPER RUSHED.
NOLA!
BY YOUR EARS AND WHISKERS, YOU'RE LATE, YOU'RE LATE, YOU'RE LATE?
MY WHISKERS??
PRETTY GIRLS DON'T HAVE WHISKERS.

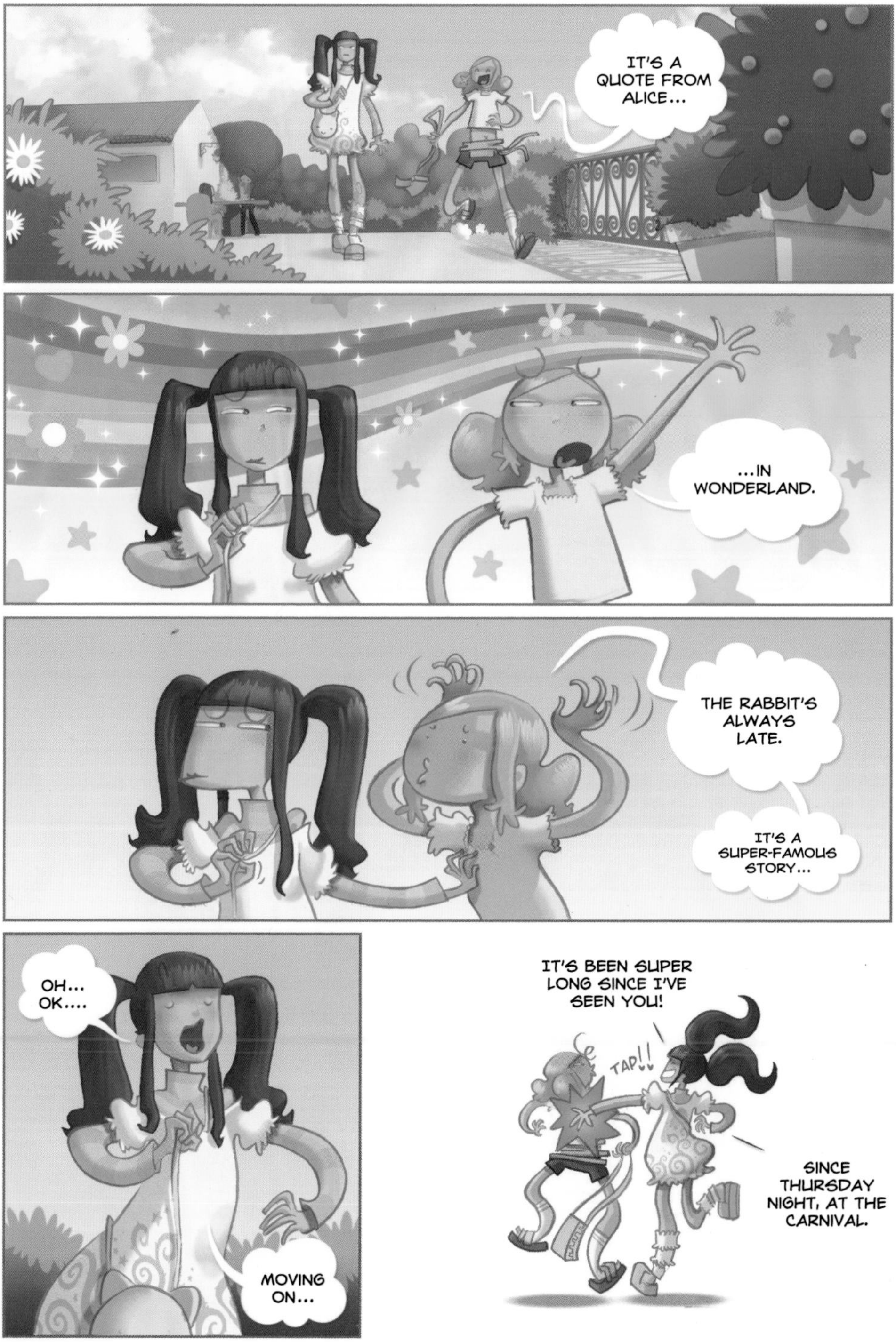
IT'S A QUOTE FROM ALICE...
...IN WONDERLAND.
THE RABBIT'S ALWAYS LATE.
IT'S A SUPER-FAMOUS STORY...
OH... OK....
MOVING ON...
IT'S BEEN SUPER LONG SINCE I'VE SEEN YOU!
TAP!!
SINCE THURSDAY NIGHT, AT THE CARNIVAL.

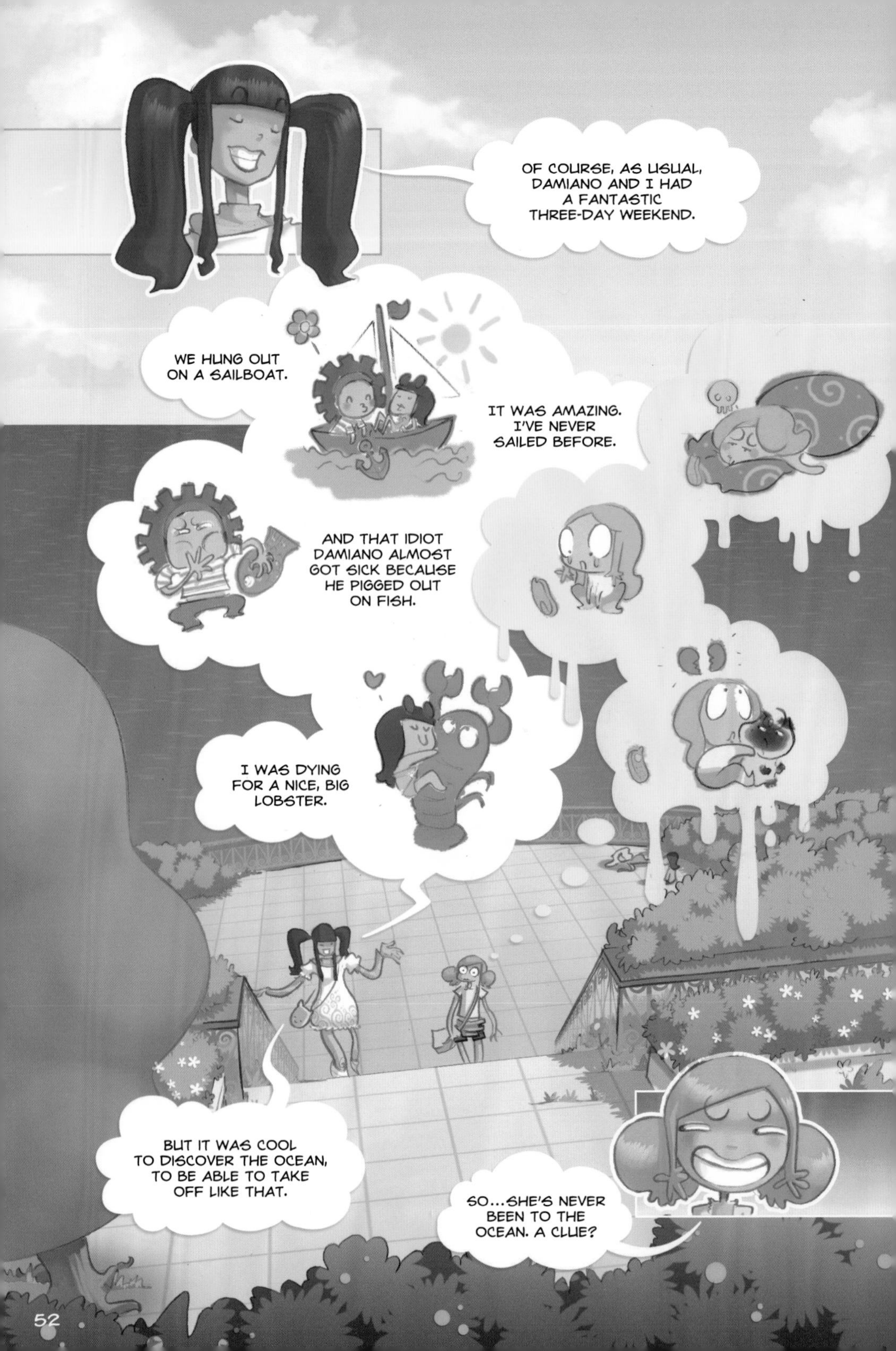
OF COURSE, AS USUAL, DAMIANO AND I HAD A FANTASTIC THREE-DAY WEEKEND.
WE HUNG OUT ON A SAILBOAT.
IT WAS AMAZING. I'VE NEVER SAILED BEFORE.
AND THAT IDIOT DAMIANO ALMOST GOT SICK BECAUSE HE PIGGED OUT ON FISH.
I WAS DYING FOR A NICE, BIG LOBSTER.
BUT IT WAS COOL TO DISCOVER THE OCEAN, TO BE ABLE TO TAKE OFF LIKE THAT.
SO...SHE'S NEVER BEEN TO THE OCEAN. A CLUE?

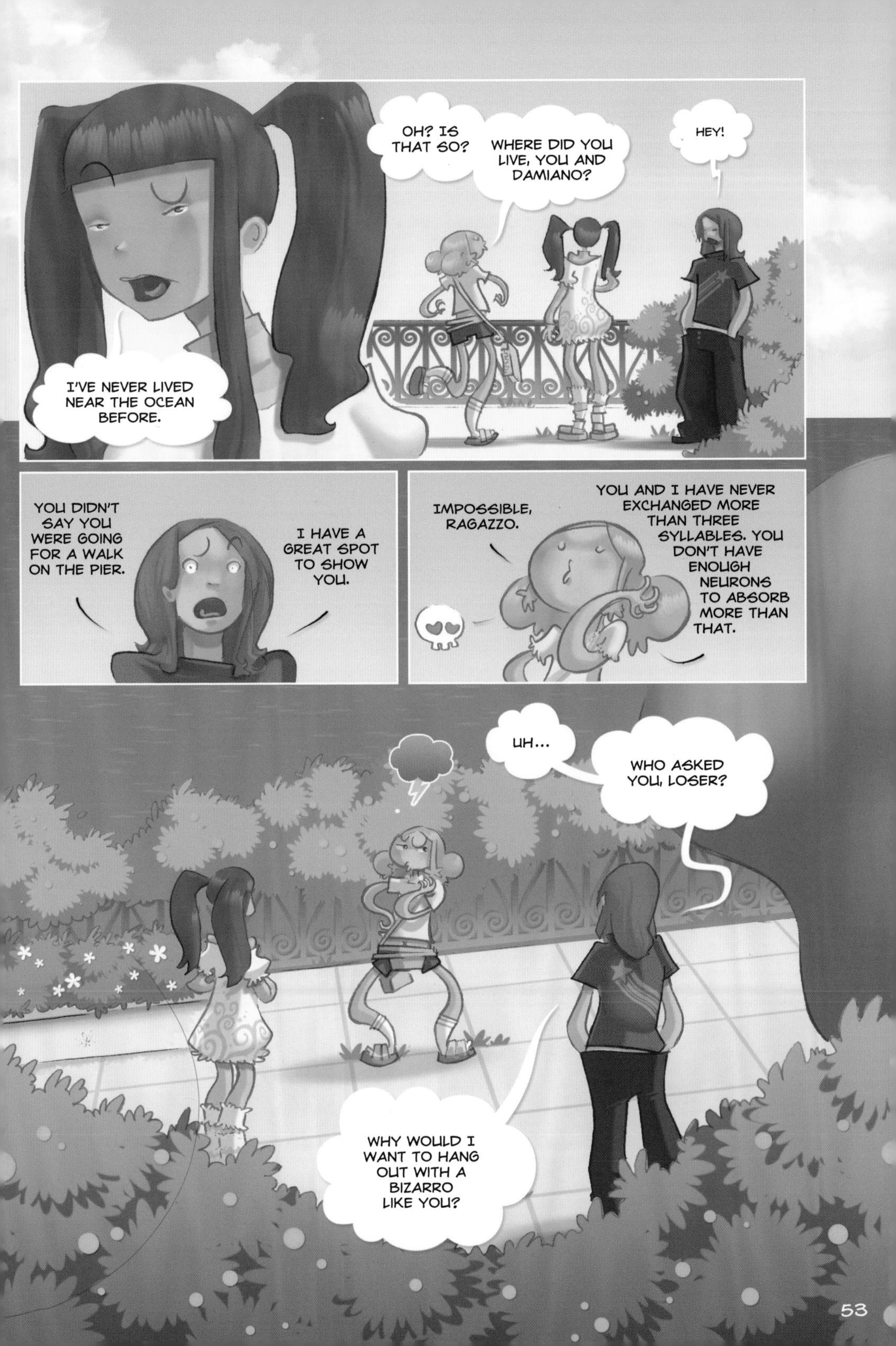
I'VE NEVER LIVED NEAR THE OCEAN BEFORE.
OH? IS THAT SO?
WHERE DID YOU LIVE, YOU AND DAMIANO?
HEY!
YOU DIDN'T SAY YOU WERE GOING FOR A WALK ON THE PIER.
I HAVE A GREAT SPOT TO SHOW YOU.
IMPOSSIBLE, RAGAZZO.
YOU AND I HAVE NEVER EXCHANGED MORE THAN THREE SYLLABLES. YOU DON'T HAVE ENOUGH NEURONS TO ABSORB MORE THAN THAT.
UH...
WHO ASKED YOU, LOSER?
WHY WOULD I WANT TO HANG OUT WITH A BIZARRO LIKE YOU?

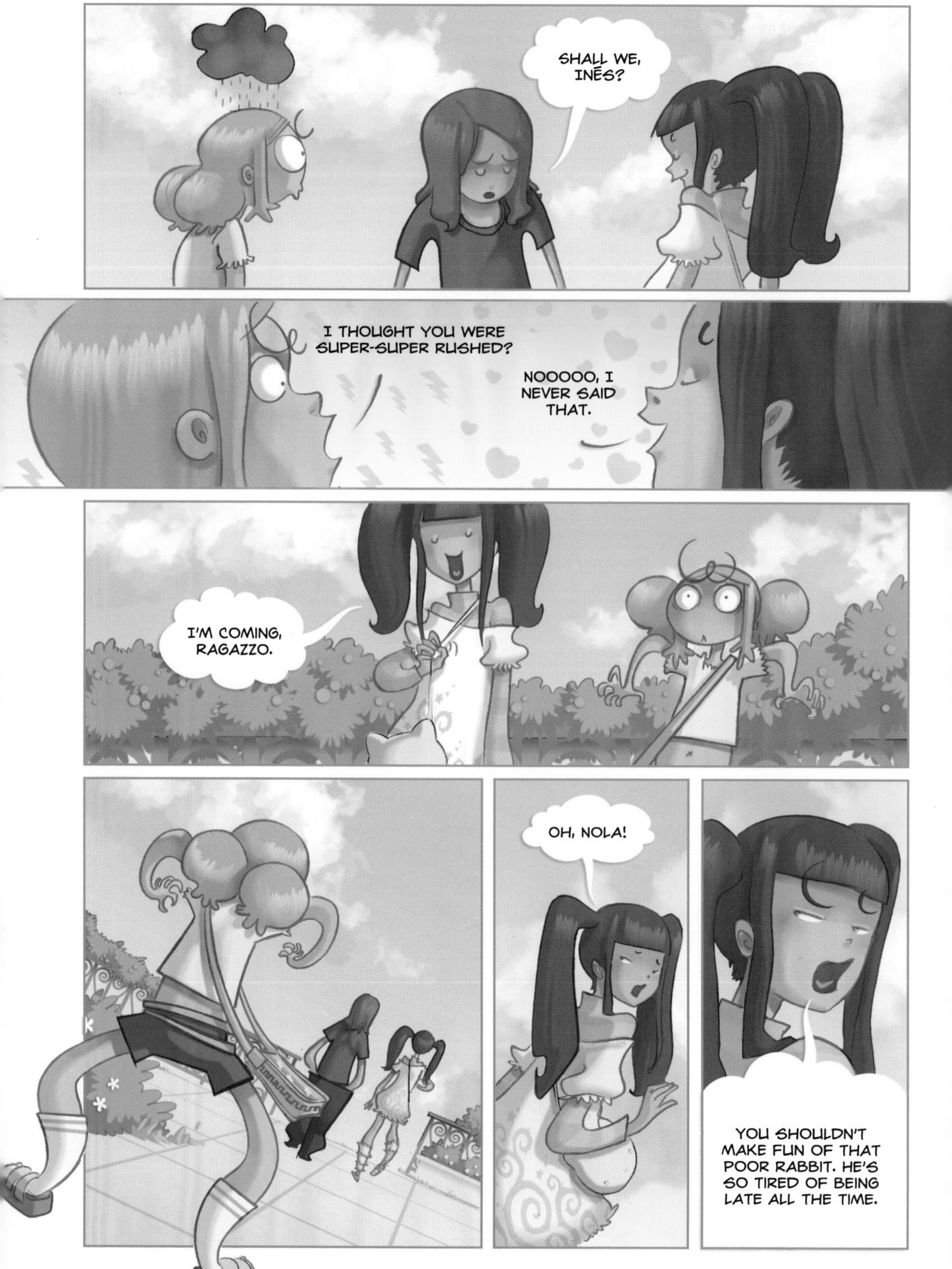
SHALL WE, INÉS?
I THOUGHT YOU WERE SUPER-SUPER RUSHED?
NOOOOO, I NEVER SAID THAT.
I'M COMING, RAGAZZO.
OH, NOLA!
YOU SHOULDN'T MAKE FUN OF THAT POOR RABBIT. HE'S SO TIRED OF BEING LATE ALL THE TIME.

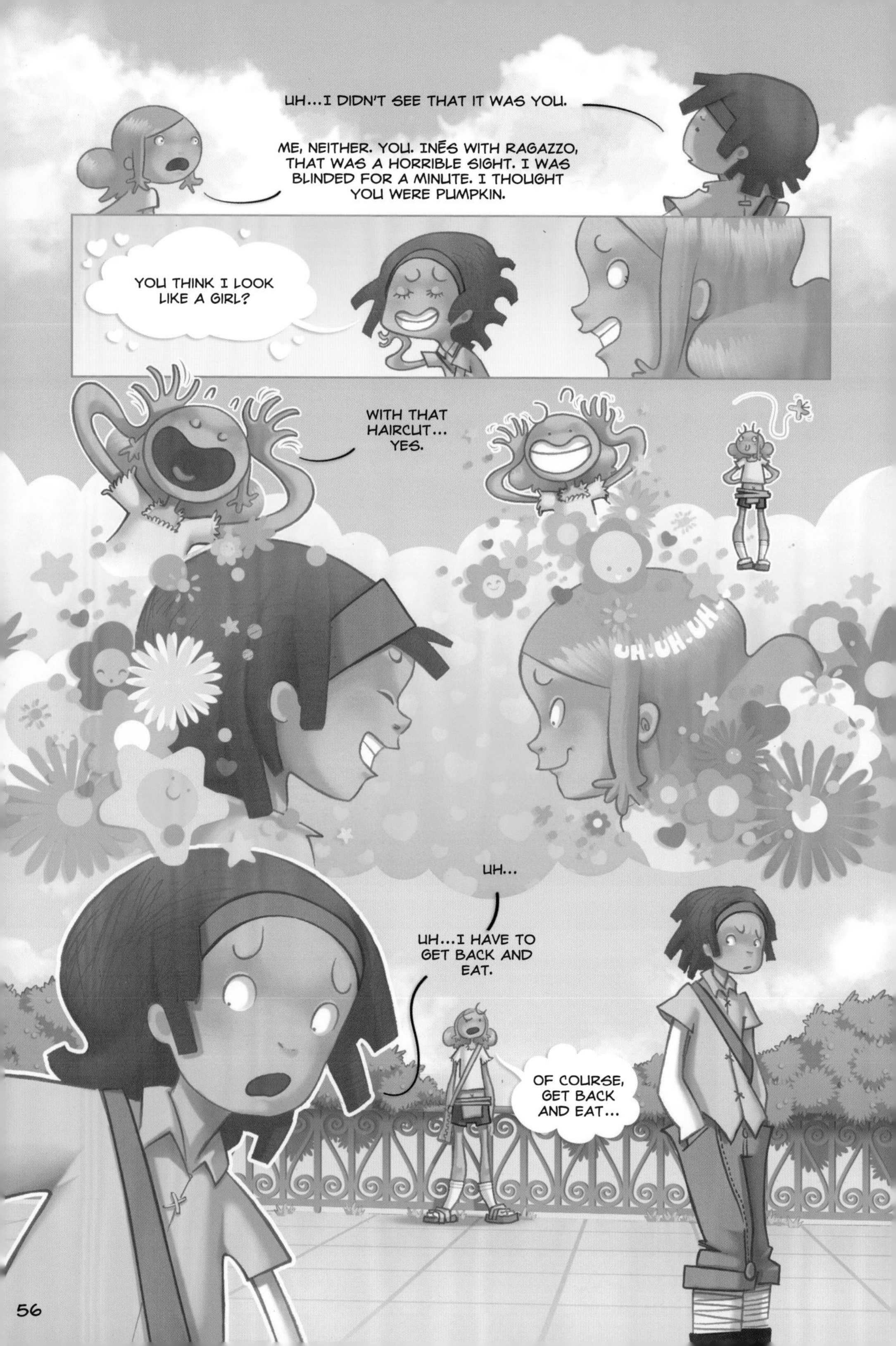
UH...I DIDN'T SEE THAT IT WAS YOU.
ME, NEITHER. YOU. INÉS WITH RAGAZZO, THAT WAS A HORRIBLE SIGHT. I WAS BLINDED FOR A MINUTE. I THOUGHT YOU WERE PUMPKIN.
YOU THINK I LOOK LIKE A GIRL?
WITH THAT HAIRCUT... YES.
UH.UH.UH...
UH...
UH...I HAVE TO GET BACK AND EAT.
OF COURSE, GET BACK AND EAT...

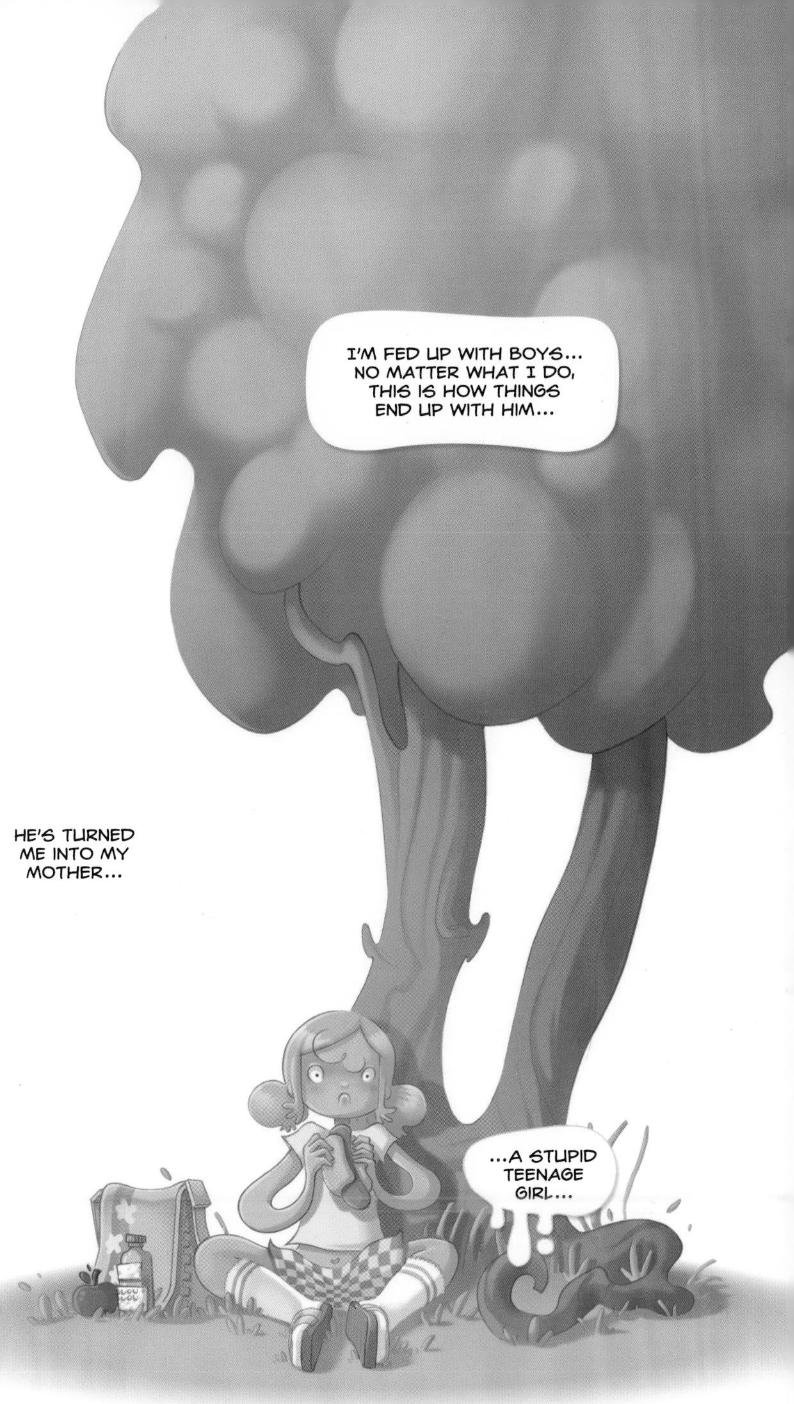
I'M FED UP WITH BOYS... NO MATTER WHAT I DO, THIS IS HOW THINGS END UP WITH HIM...
HE'S TURNED ME INTO MY MOTHER...
...A STUPID TEENAGE GIRL...

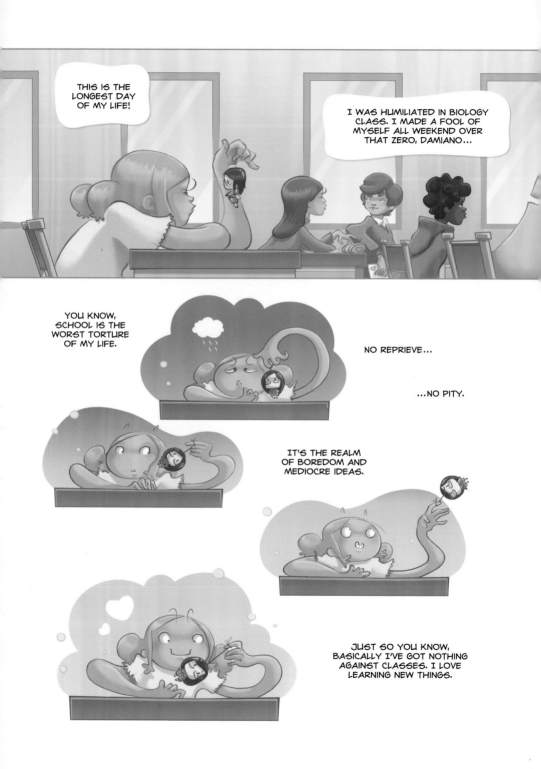

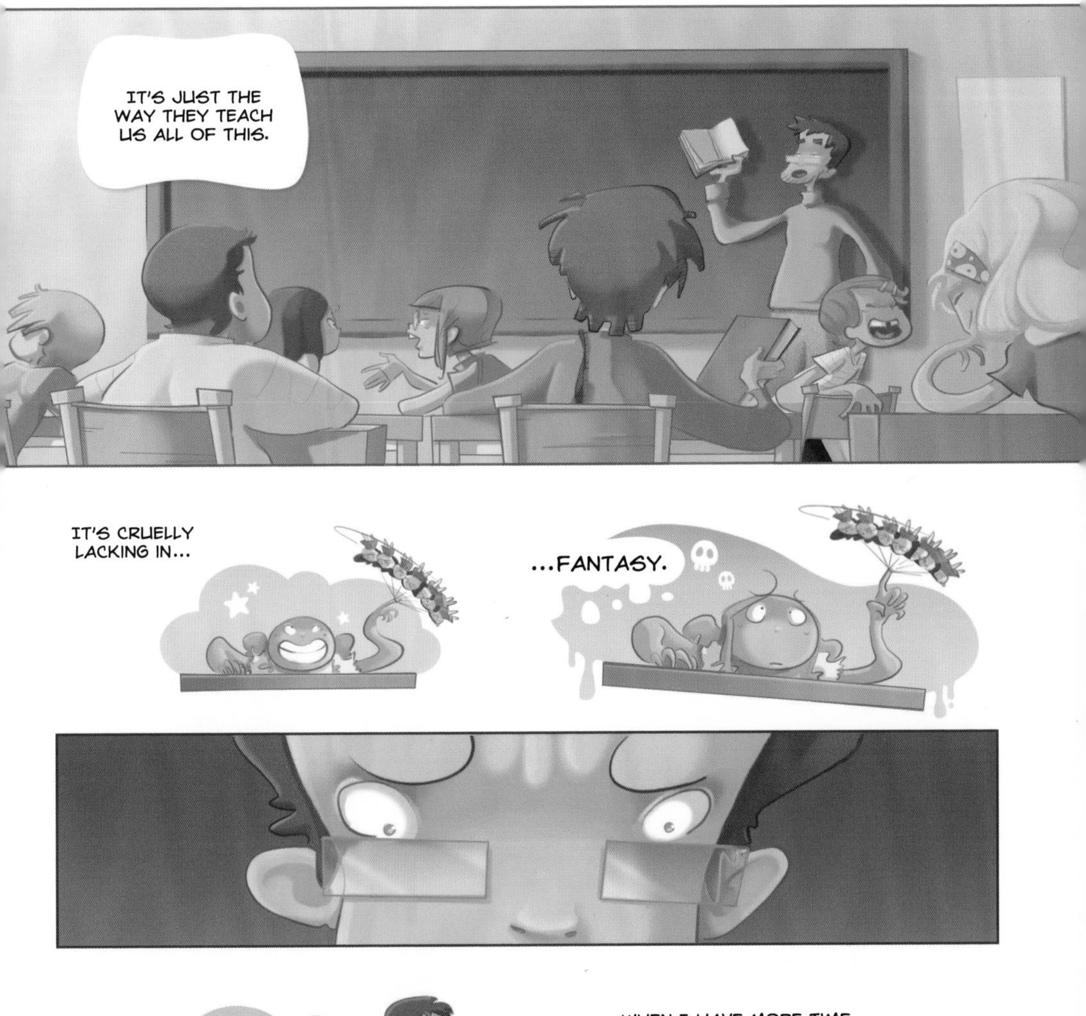
IT'S JUST THE WAY THEY TEACH US ALL OF THIS.
IT'S CRUELLY LACKING IN...
...FANTASY.
WHEN I HAVE MORE TIME, I'LL TELL YOU HOW MY HISTORY TEACHER TEACHES US ABOUT WARS.
AND I'LL EXPLAIN HOW I'D DO IT BETTER THAN HE DOES.

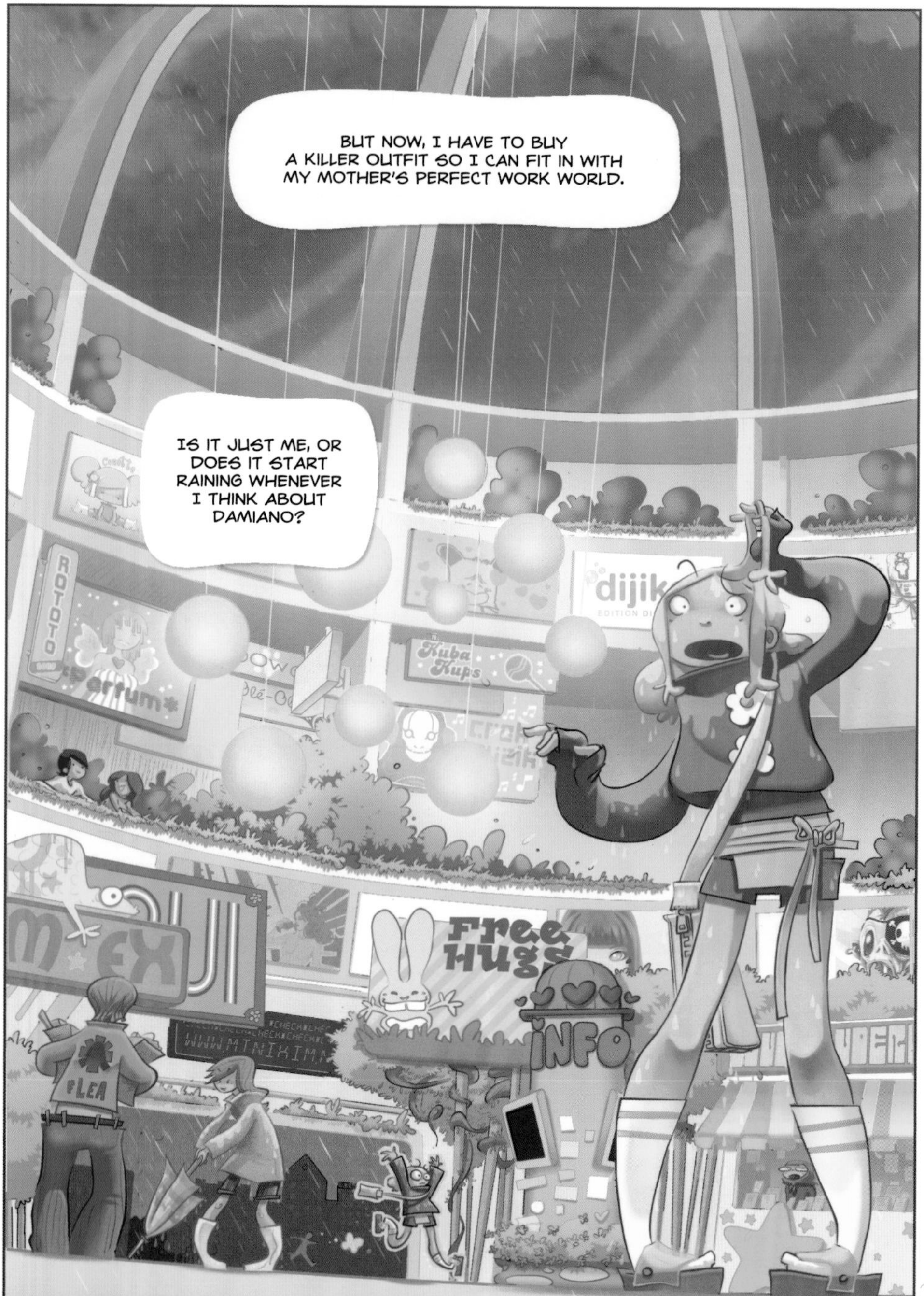
BUT NOW, I HAVE TO BUY A KILLER OUTFIT SO I CAN FIT IN WITH MY MOTHER'S PERFECT WORK WORLD.
IS IT JUST ME, OR DOES IT START RAINING WHENEVER I THINK ABOUT DAMIANO?
ROTOTO
Parfum
dijik
Kuba Kups
Free HUGS
INFO
FLEA

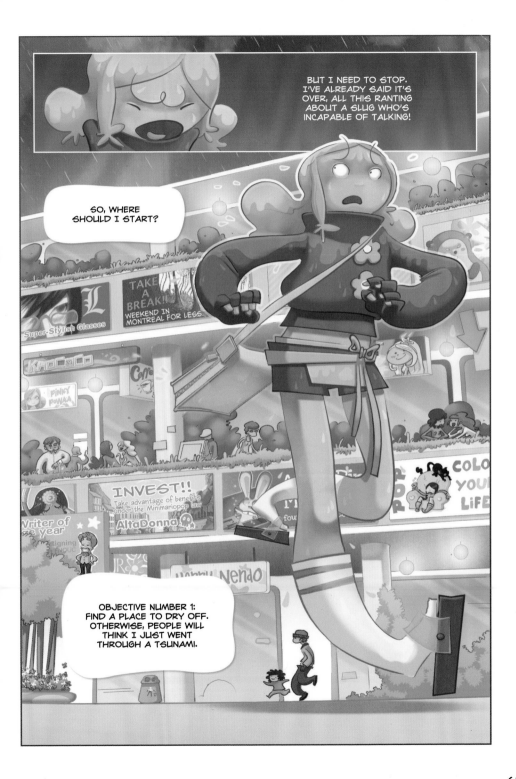

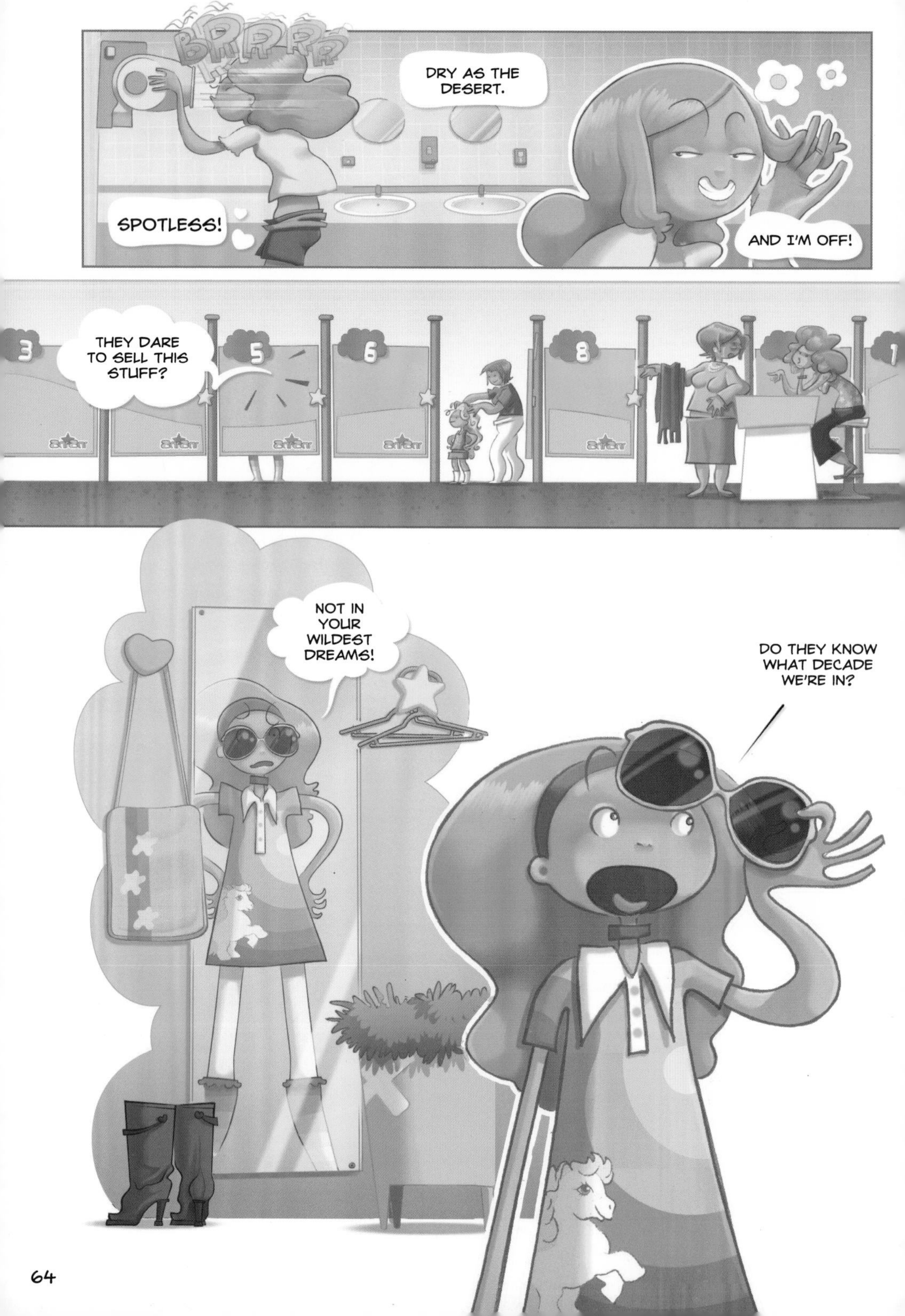
SPOTLESS!
DRY AS THE DESERT.
AND I'M OFF!
THEY DARE TO SELL THIS STUFF?
NOT IN YOUR WILDEST DREAMS!
DO THEY KNOW WHAT DECADE WE'RE IN?

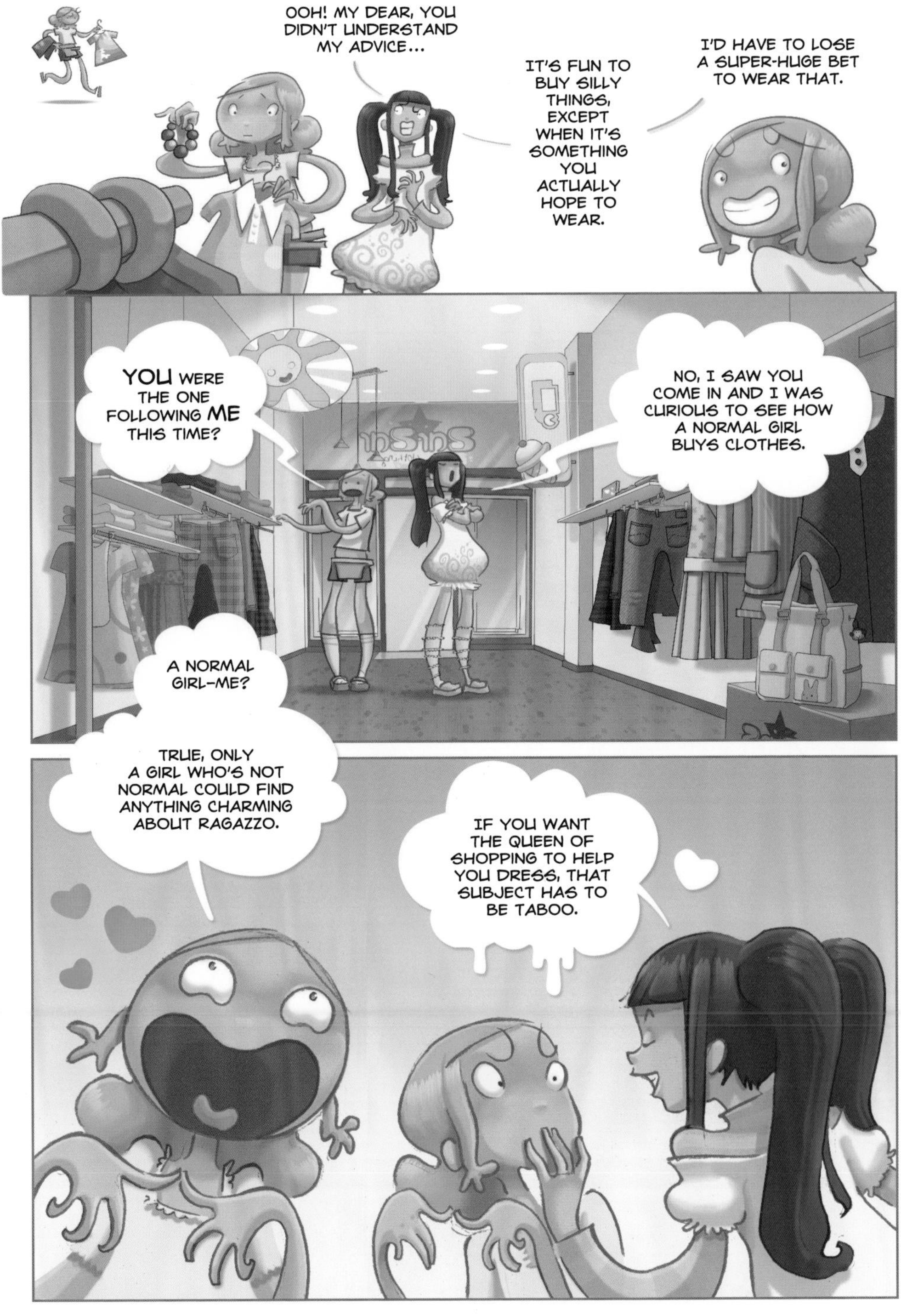
OOH! MY DEAR, YOU DIDN'T UNDERSTAND MY ADVICE...
IT'S FUN TO BUY SILLY THINGS, EXCEPT WHEN IT'S SOMETHING YOU ACTUALLY HOPE TO WEAR.
I'D HAVE TO LOSE A SUPER-HUGE BET TO WEAR THAT.
YOU WERE THE ONE FOLLOWING ME THIS TIME?
NO, I SAW YOU COME IN AND I WAS CURIOUS TO SEE HOW A NORMAL GIRL BUYS CLOTHES.
A NORMAL GIRL–ME?
TRUE, ONLY A GIRL WHO'S NOT NORMAL COULD FIND ANYTHING CHARMING ABOUT RAGAZZO.
IF YOU WANT THE QUEEN OF SHOPPING TO HELP YOU DRESS, THAT SUBJECT HAS TO BE TABOO.

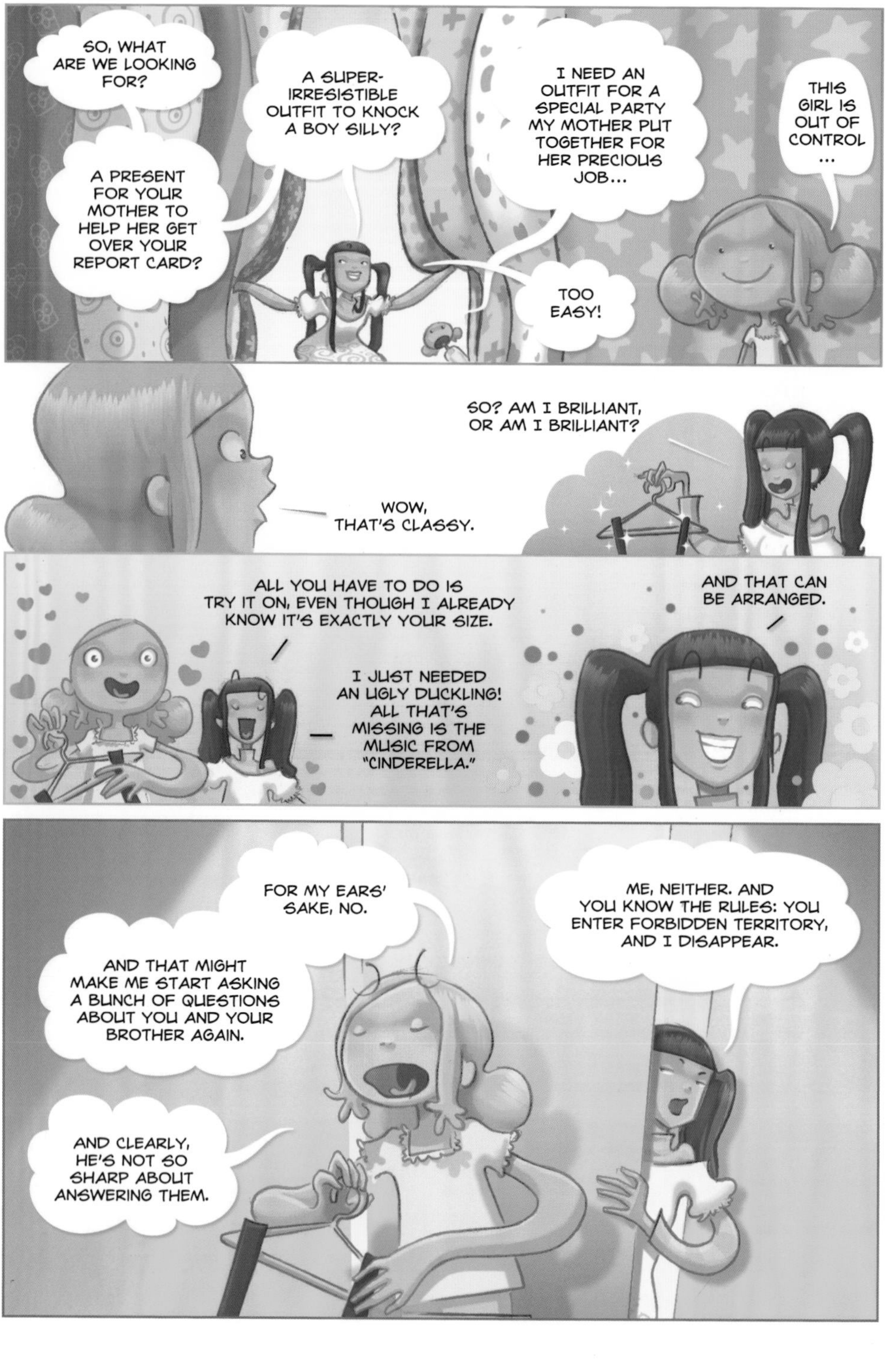

SO, WHAT ARE WE LOOKING FOR?
A PRESENT FOR YOUR MOTHER TO HELP HER GET OVER YOUR REPORT CARD?
A SUPER-IRRESISTIBLE OUTFIT TO KNOCK A BOY SILLY?
I NEED AN OUTFIT FOR A SPECIAL PARTY MY MOTHER PUT TOGETHER FOR HER PRECIOUS JOB...
TOO EASY!
THIS GIRL IS OUT OF CONTROL ...
SO? AM I BRILLIANT, OR AM I BRILLIANT?
WOW, THAT'S CLASSY.
ALL YOU HAVE TO DO IS TRY IT ON, EVEN THOUGH I ALREADY KNOW IT'S EXACTLY YOUR SIZE.
I JUST NEEDED AN UGLY DUCKLING! ALL THAT'S MISSING IS THE MUSIC FROM "CINDERELLA."
AND THAT CAN BE ARRANGED.
FOR MY EARS' SAKE, NO.
AND THAT MIGHT MAKE ME START ASKING A BUNCH OF QUESTIONS ABOUT YOU AND YOUR BROTHER AGAIN.
AND CLEARLY, HE'S NOT SO SHARP ABOUT ANSWERING THEM.
ME, NEITHER. AND YOU KNOW THE RULES: YOU ENTER FORBIDDEN TERRITORY, AND I DISAPPEAR.

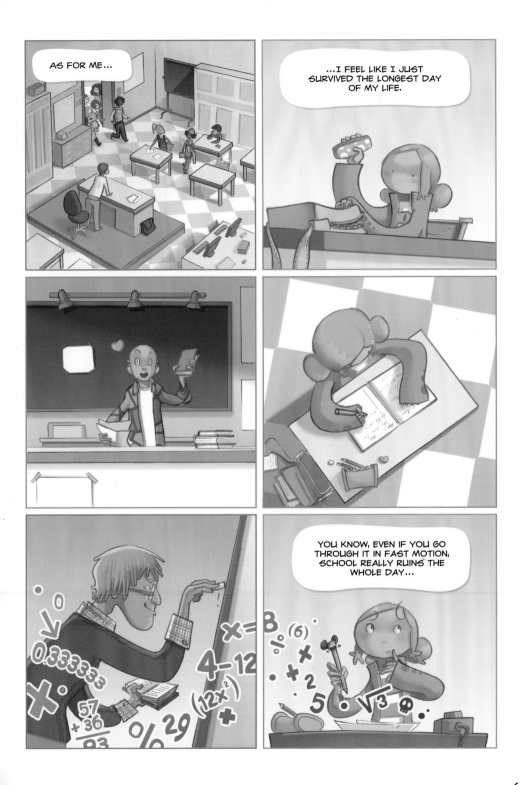

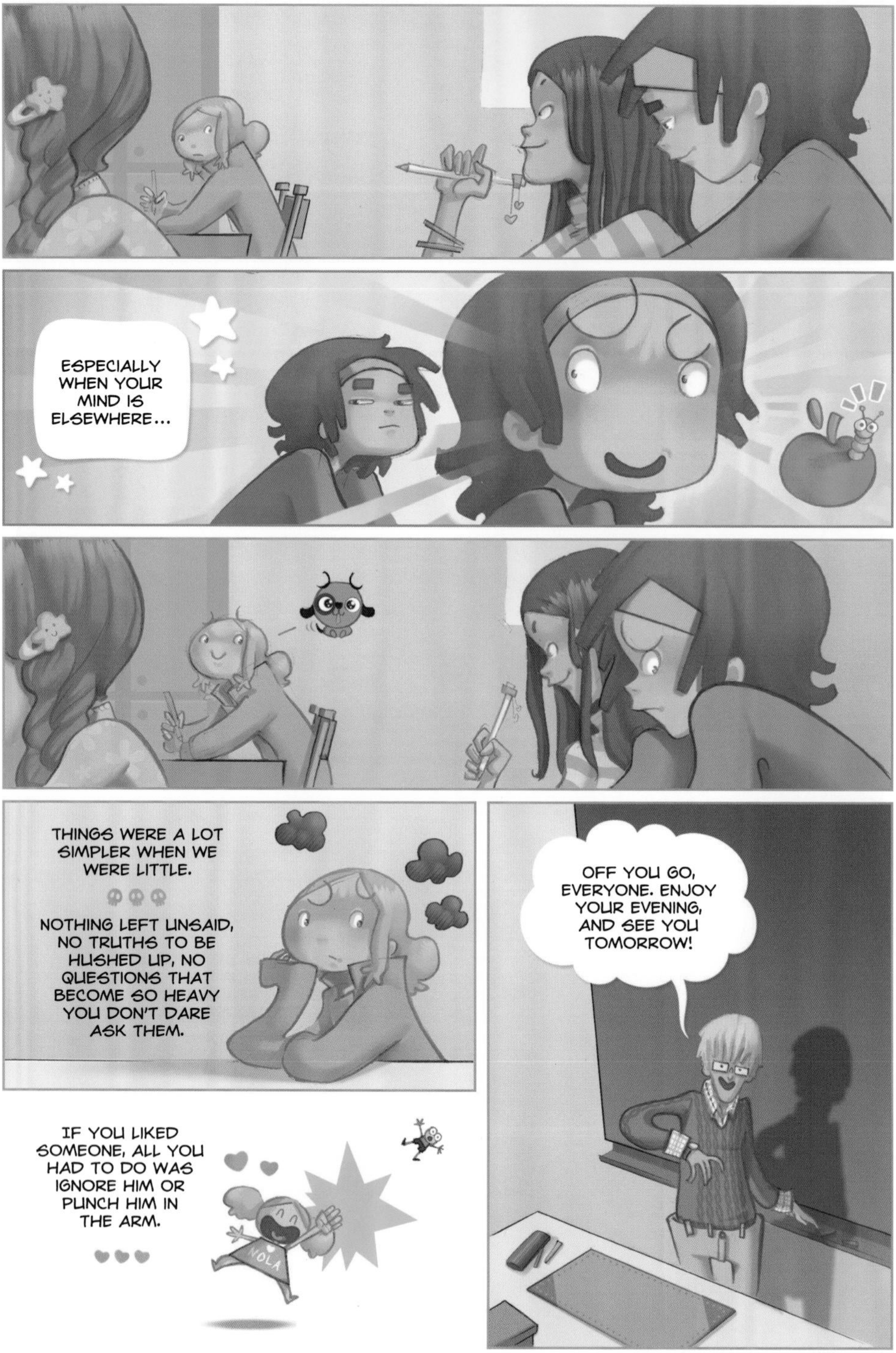
ESPECIALLY WHEN YOUR MIND IS ELSEWHERE...
THINGS WERE A LOT SIMPLER WHEN WE WERE LITTLE.
NOTHING LEFT UNSAID, NO TRUTHS TO BE HUSHED UP, NO QUESTIONS THAT BECOME SO HEAVY YOU DON'T DARE ASK THEM.
IF YOU LIKED SOMEONE, ALL YOU HAD TO DO WAS IGNORE HIM OR PUNCH HIM IN THE ARM.
NOLA
OFF YOU GO, EVERYONE. ENJOY YOUR EVENING, AND SEE YOU TOMORROW!

74

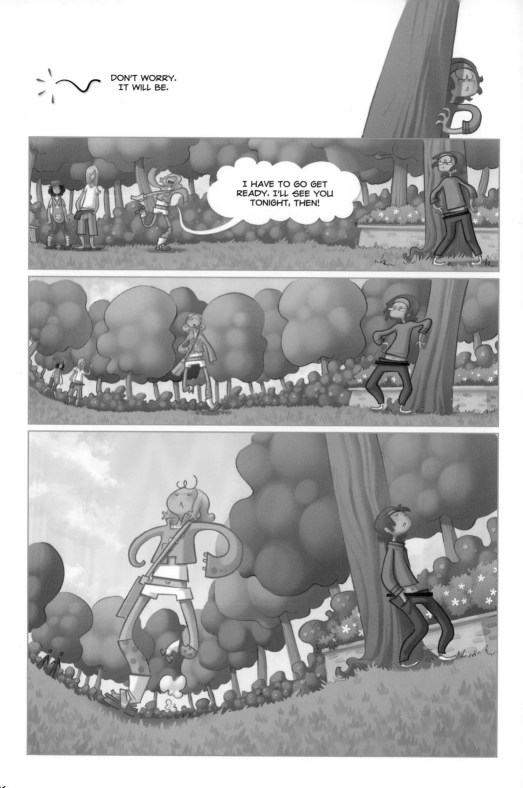

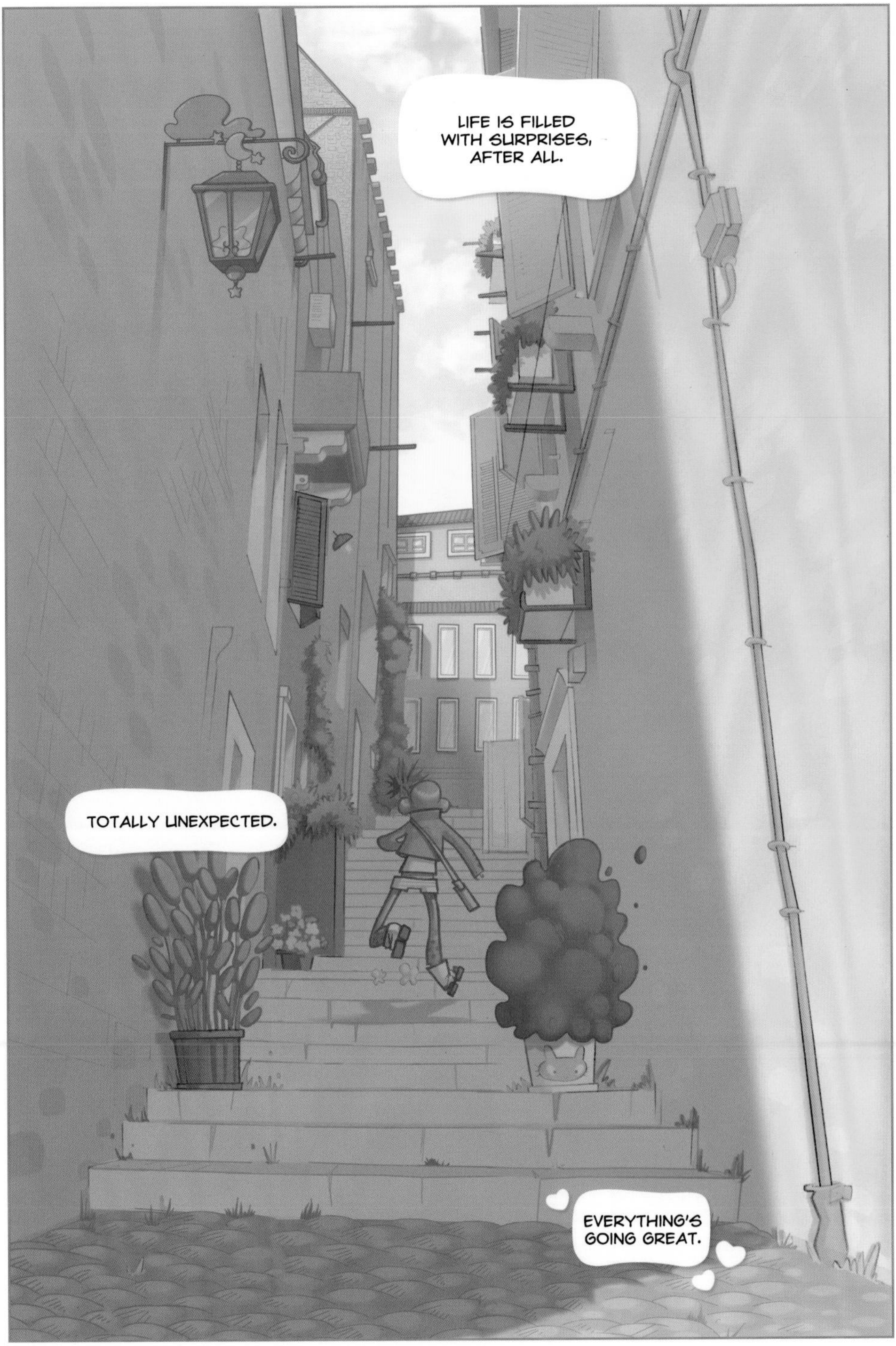
LIFE IS FILLED WITH SURPRISES, AFTER ALL.
TOTALLY UNEXPECTED.
EVERYTHING'S GOING GREAT.

79

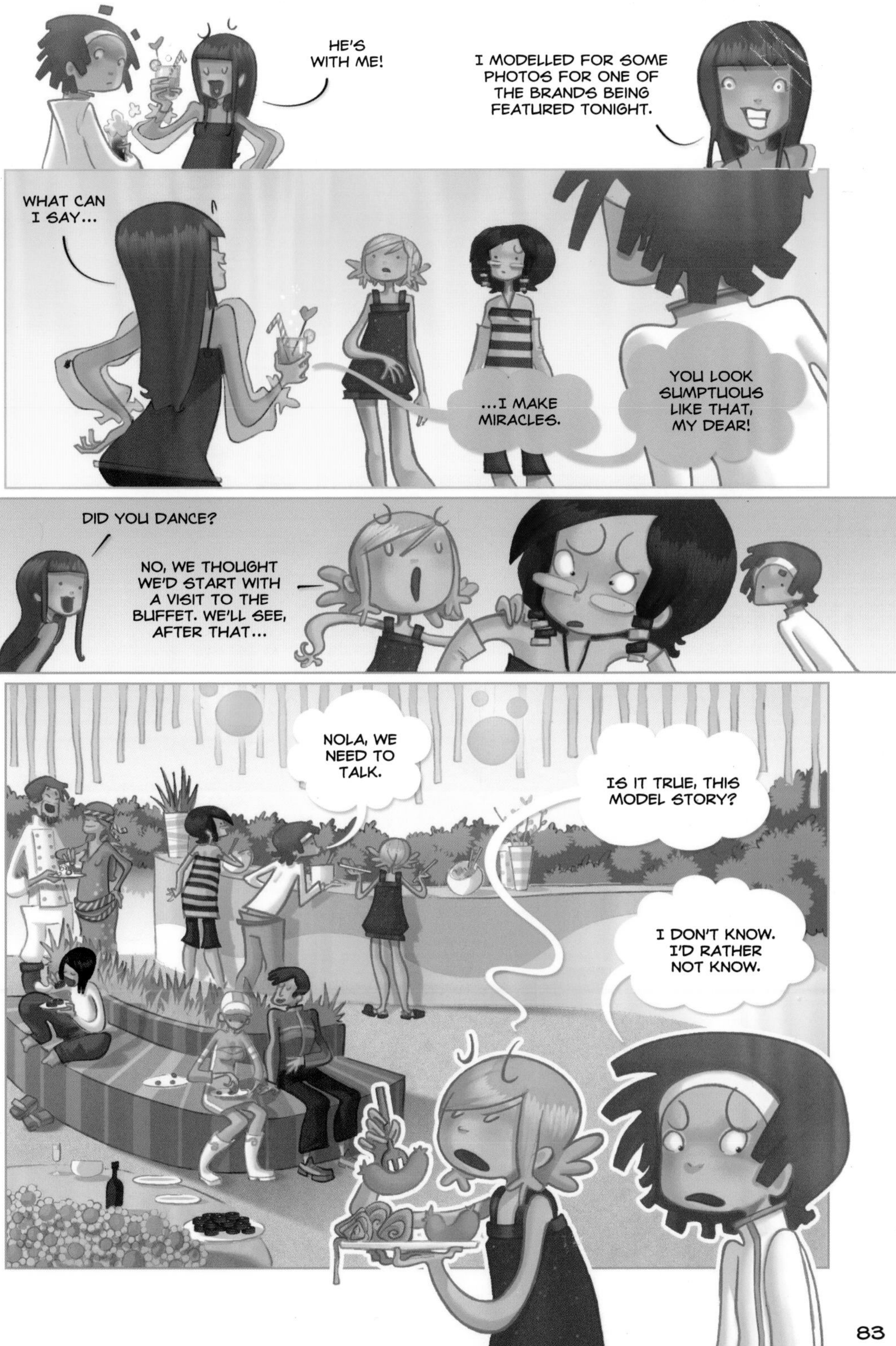
HE'S WITH ME!
I MODELLED FOR SOME PHOTOS FOR ONE OF THE BRANDS BEING FEATURED TONIGHT.
WHAT CAN I SAY...
...I MAKE MIRACLES.
YOU LOOK SUMPTUOUS LIKE THAT, MY DEAR!
DID YOU DANCE?
NO, WE THOUGHT WE'D START WITH A VISIT TO THE BUFFET. WE'LL SEE, AFTER THAT...
NOLA, WE NEED TO TALK.
IS IT TRUE, THIS MODEL STORY?
I DON'T KNOW. I'D RATHER NOT KNOW.

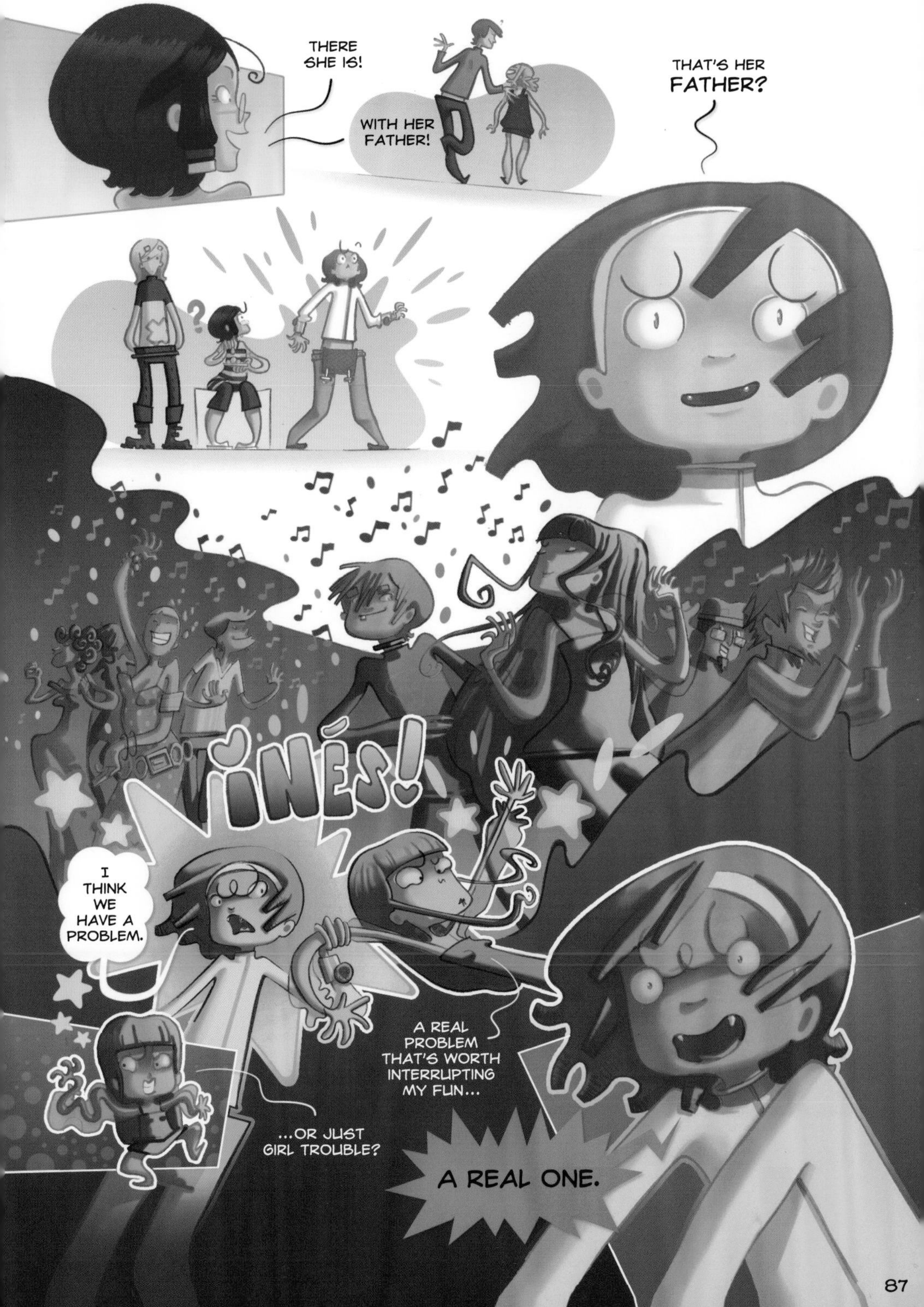

THERE SHE IS!
WITH HER FATHER!
THAT'S HER FATHER?
INÉS!
I THINK WE HAVE A PROBLEM.
A REAL PROBLEM THAT'S WORTH INTERRUPTING MY FUN...
...OR JUST GIRL TROUBLE?
A REAL ONE.

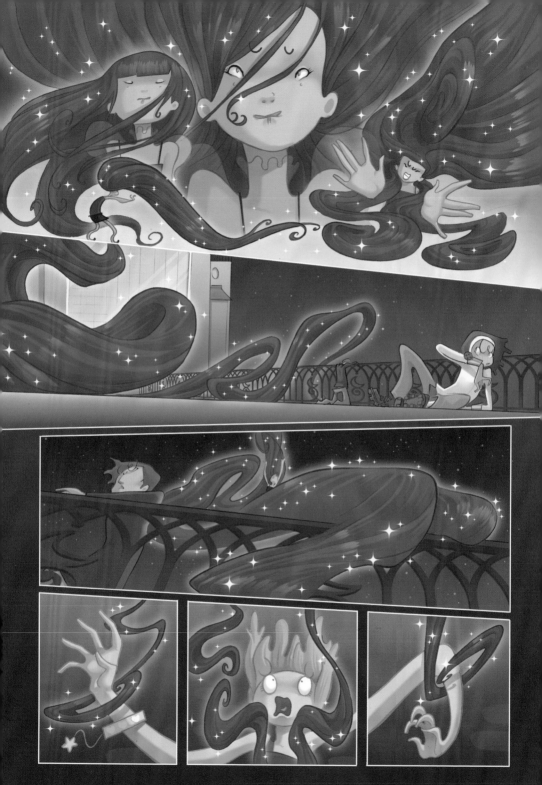

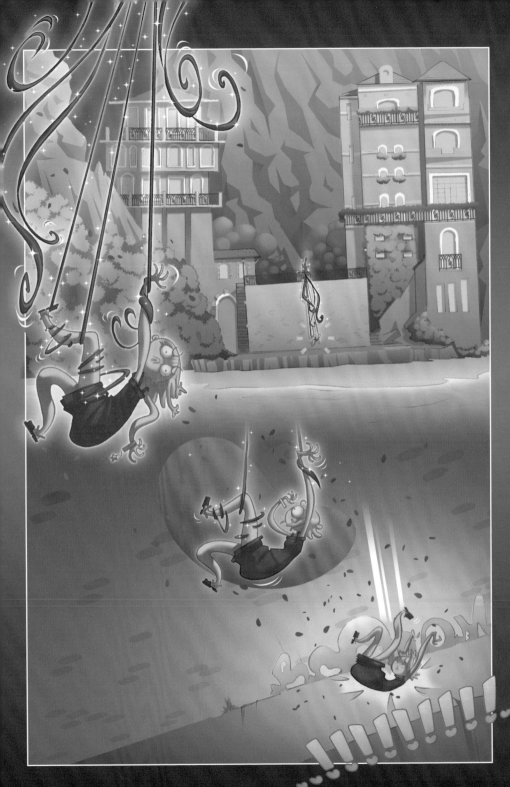

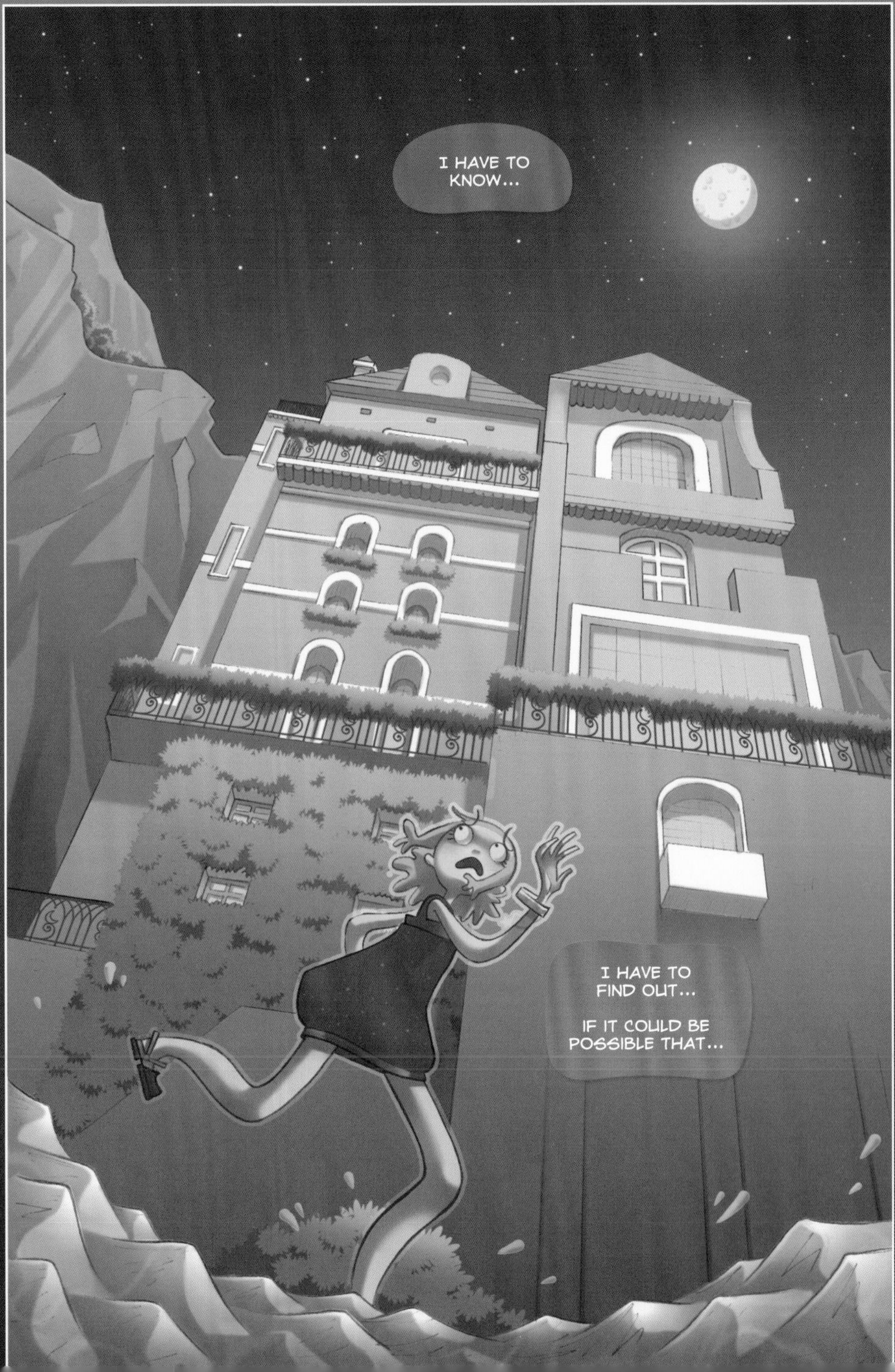
I HAVE TO KNOW...
I HAVE TO FIND OUT...
IF IT COULD BE POSSIBLE THAT...

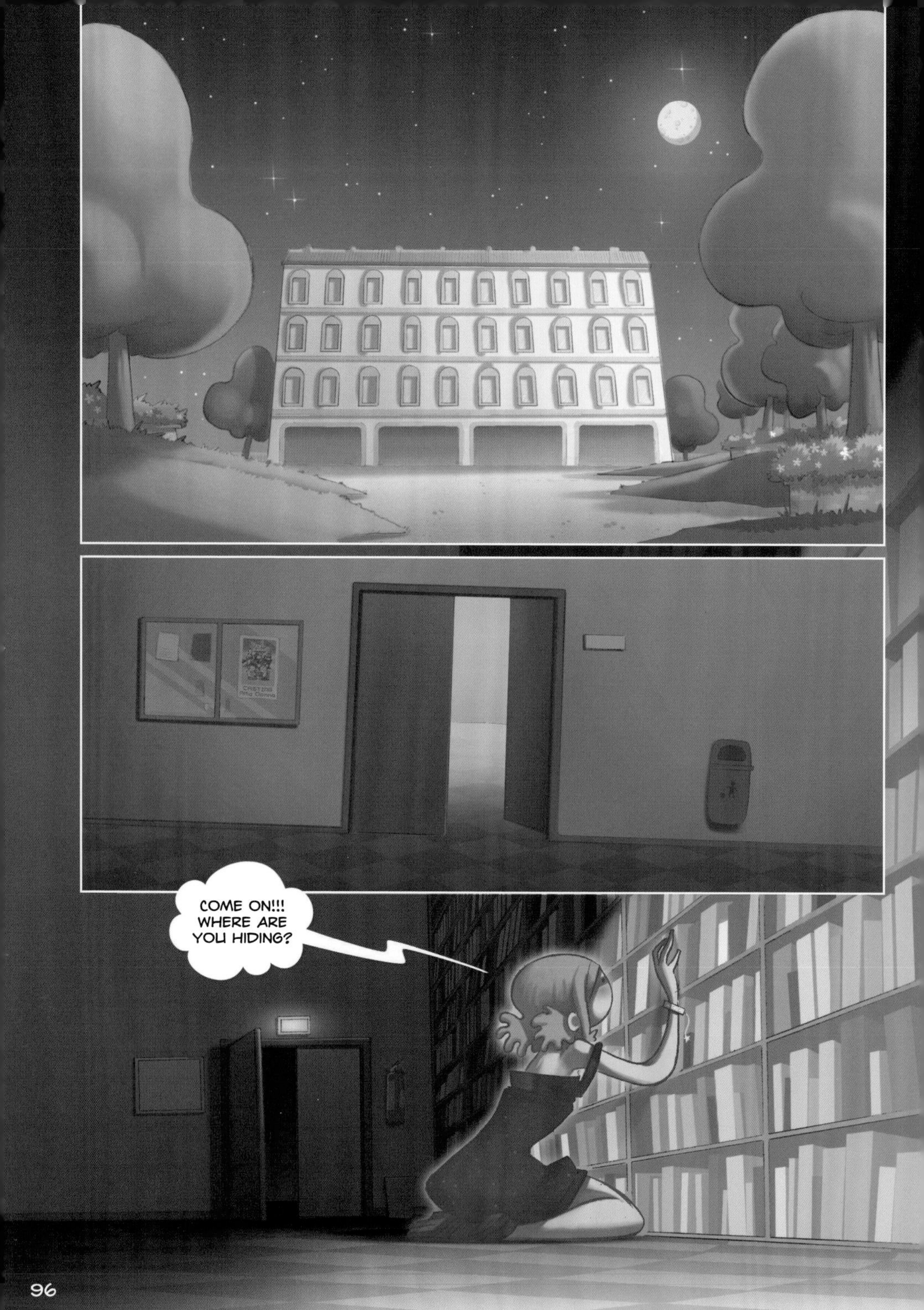
COME ON!!! WHERE ARE YOU HIDING?

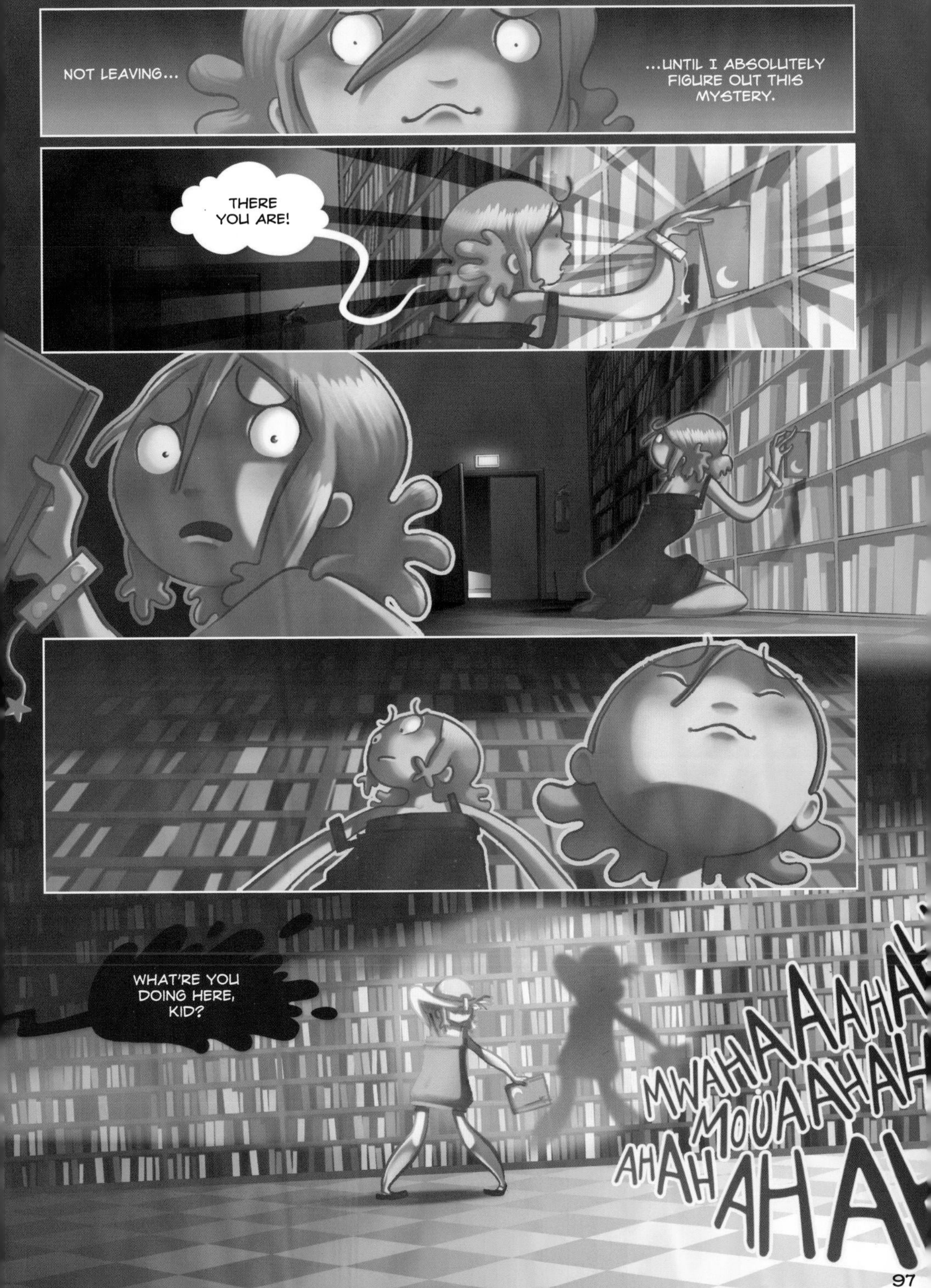
NOT LEAVING...
...UNTIL I ABSOLUTELY FIGURE OUT THIS MYSTERY.
THERE YOU ARE!
WHAT'RE YOU DOING HERE, KID?
MWAHAAAAHAH
MOUAAHAH
AHAH AHAH

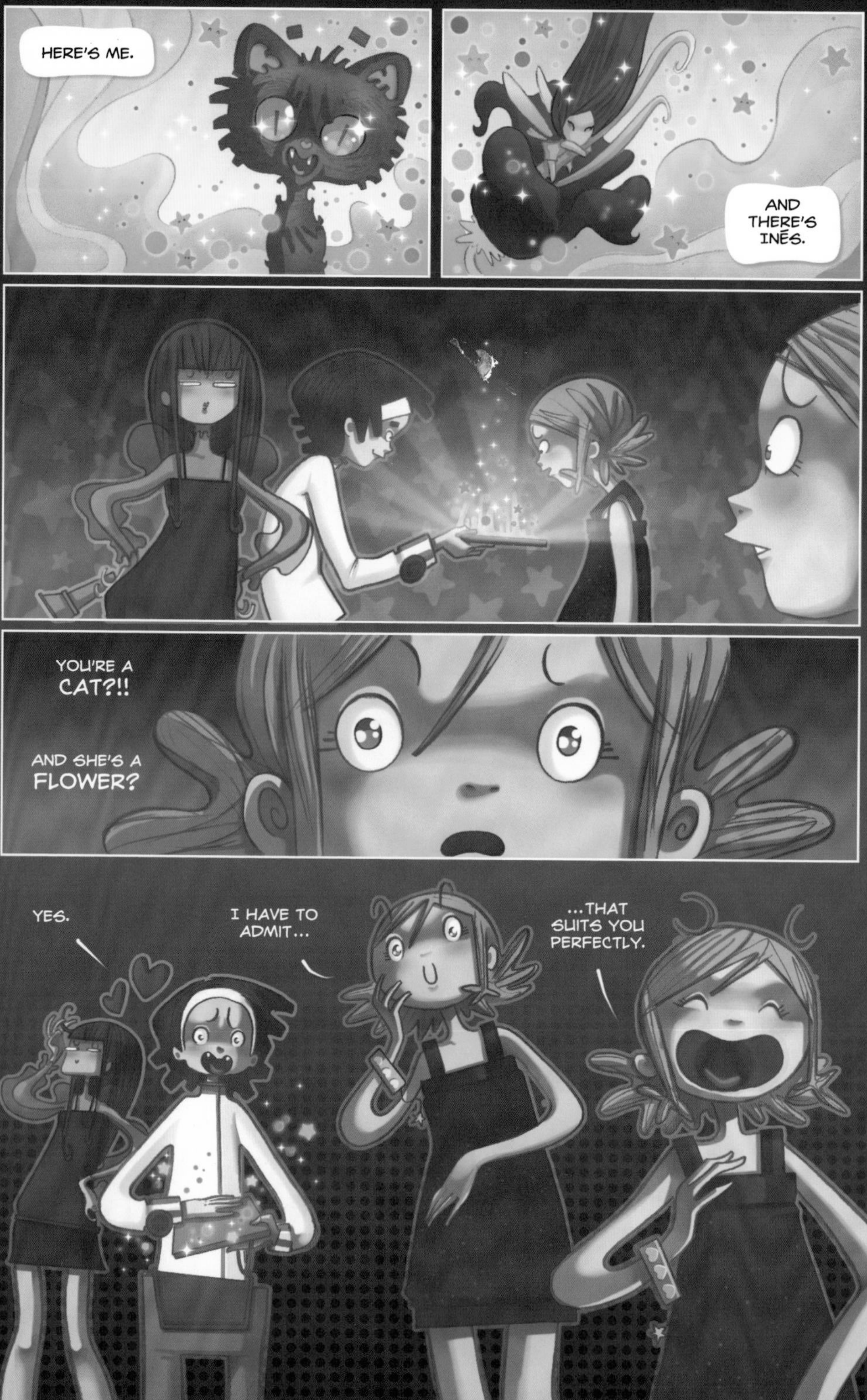
HERE'S ME.
AND THERE'S INÉS.
YOU'RE A CAT?!!
AND SHE'S A FLOWER?
YES.
I HAVE TO ADMIT...
...THAT SUITS YOU PERFECTLY.

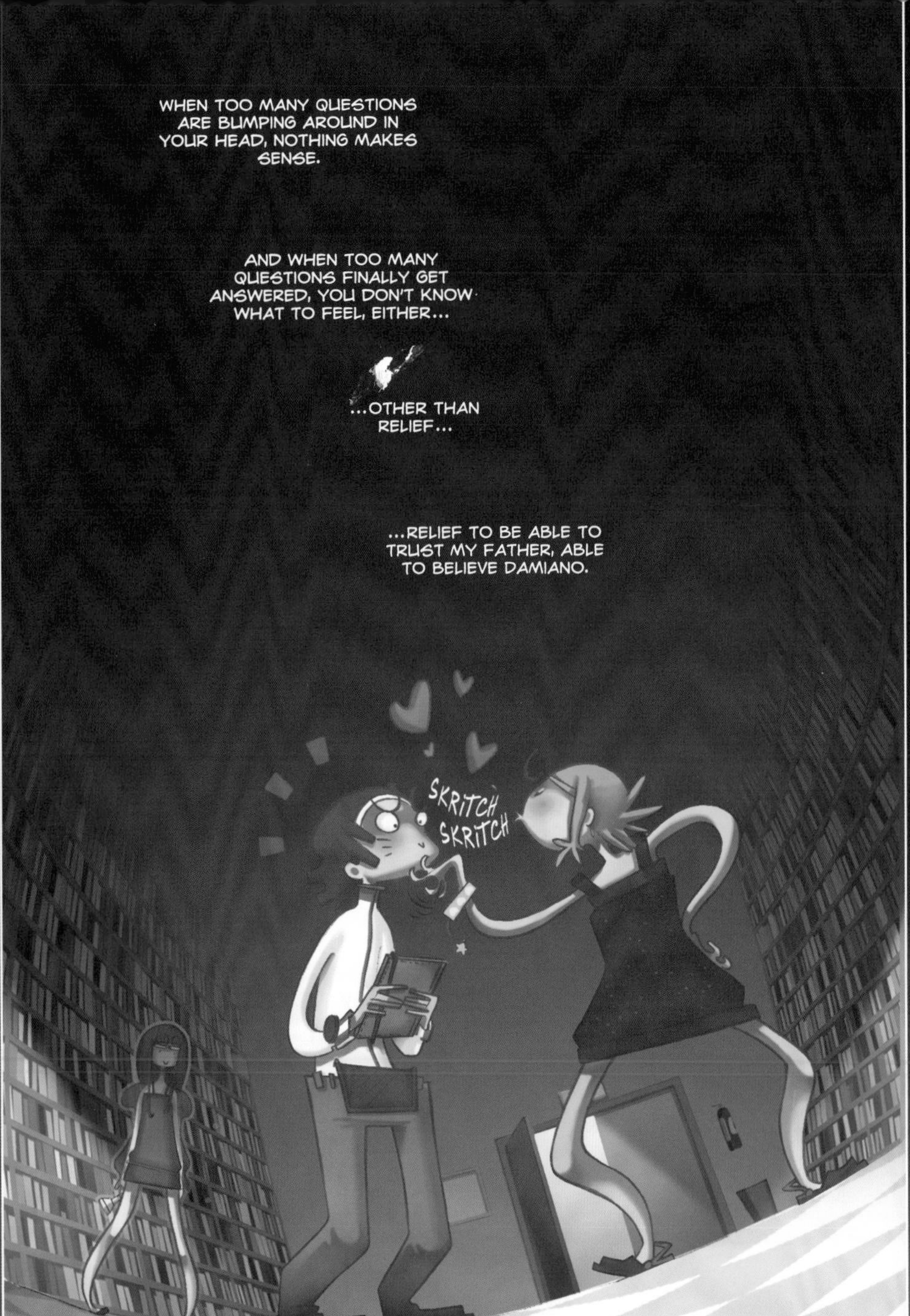
WHEN TOO MANY QUESTIONS ARE BUMPING AROUND IN YOUR HEAD, NOTHING MAKES SENSE.
AND WHEN TOO MANY QUESTIONS FINALLY GET ANSWERED, YOU DON'T KNOW WHAT TO FEEL, EITHER...
...OTHER THAN RELIEF...
...RELIEF TO BE ABLE TO TRUST MY FATHER, ABLE TO BELIEVE DAMIANO.
SKRITCH SKRITCH

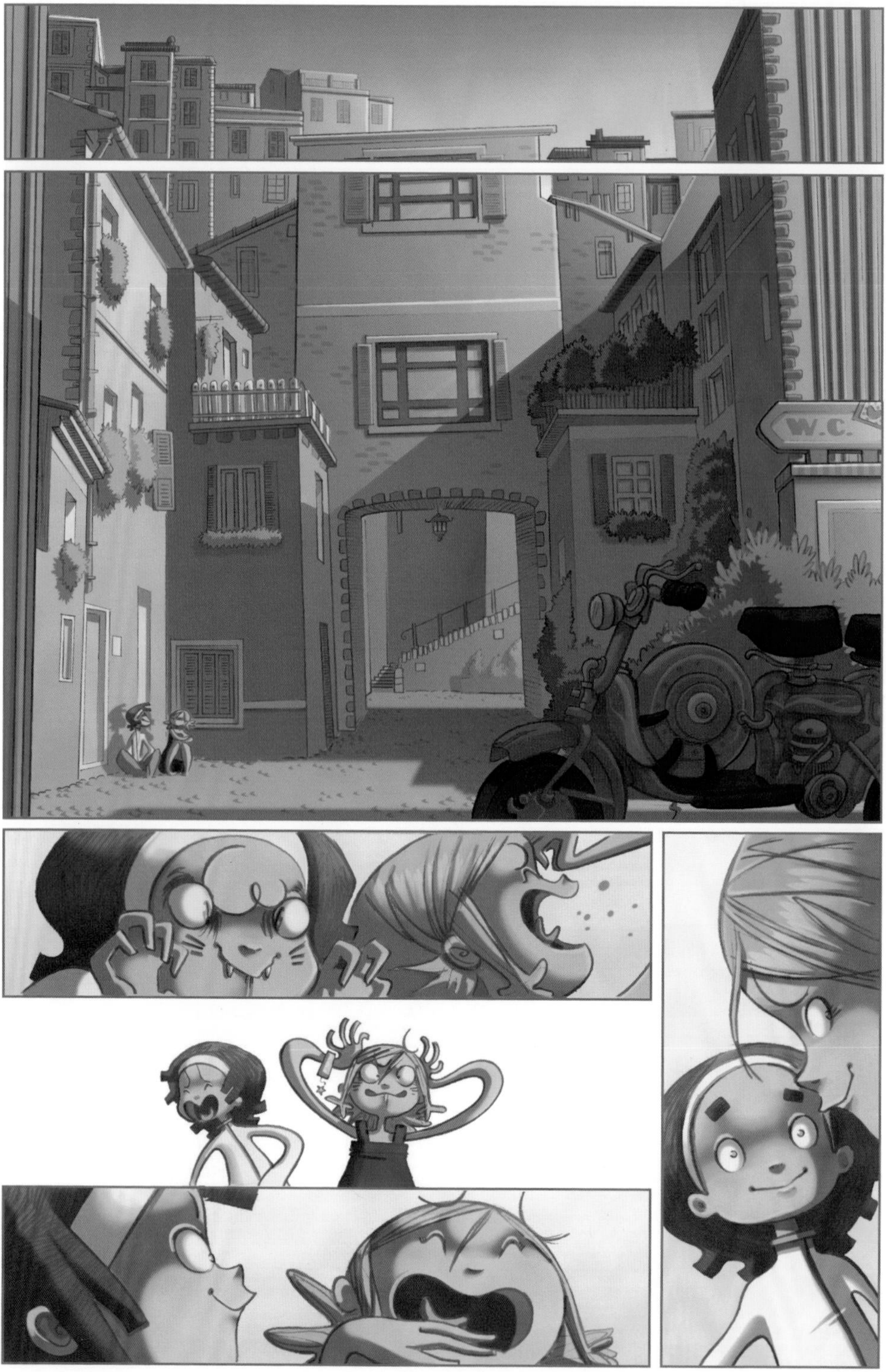
W.C.

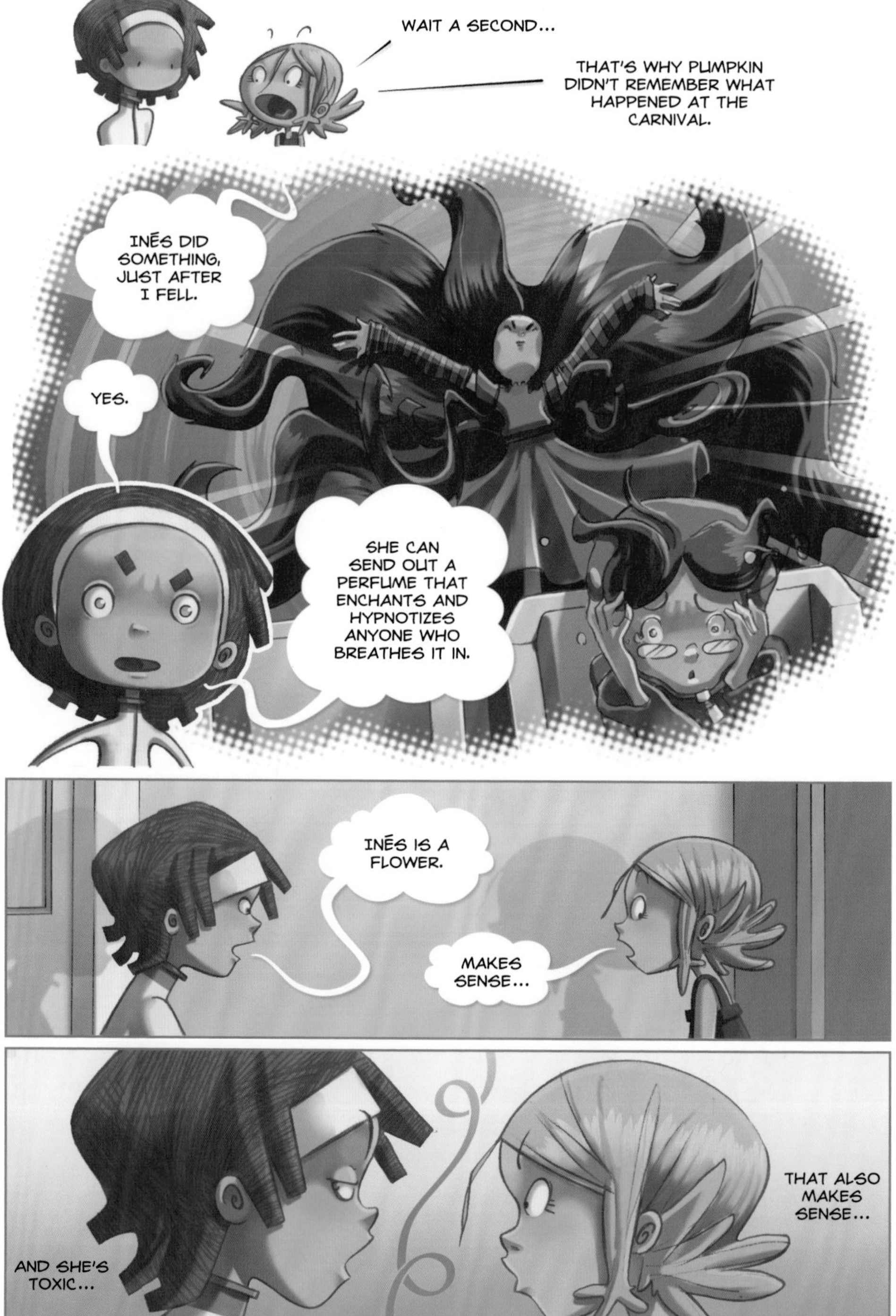
WAIT A SECOND...
THAT'S WHY PUMPKIN DIDN'T REMEMBER WHAT HAPPENED AT THE CARNIVAL.
INÉS DID SOMETHING, JUST AFTER I FELL.
YES.
SHE CAN SEND OUT A PERFUME THAT ENCHANTS AND HYPNOTIZES ANYONE WHO BREATHES IT IN.
INÉS IS A FLOWER.
MAKES SENSE...
AND SHE'S TOXIC...
THAT ALSO MAKES SENSE...

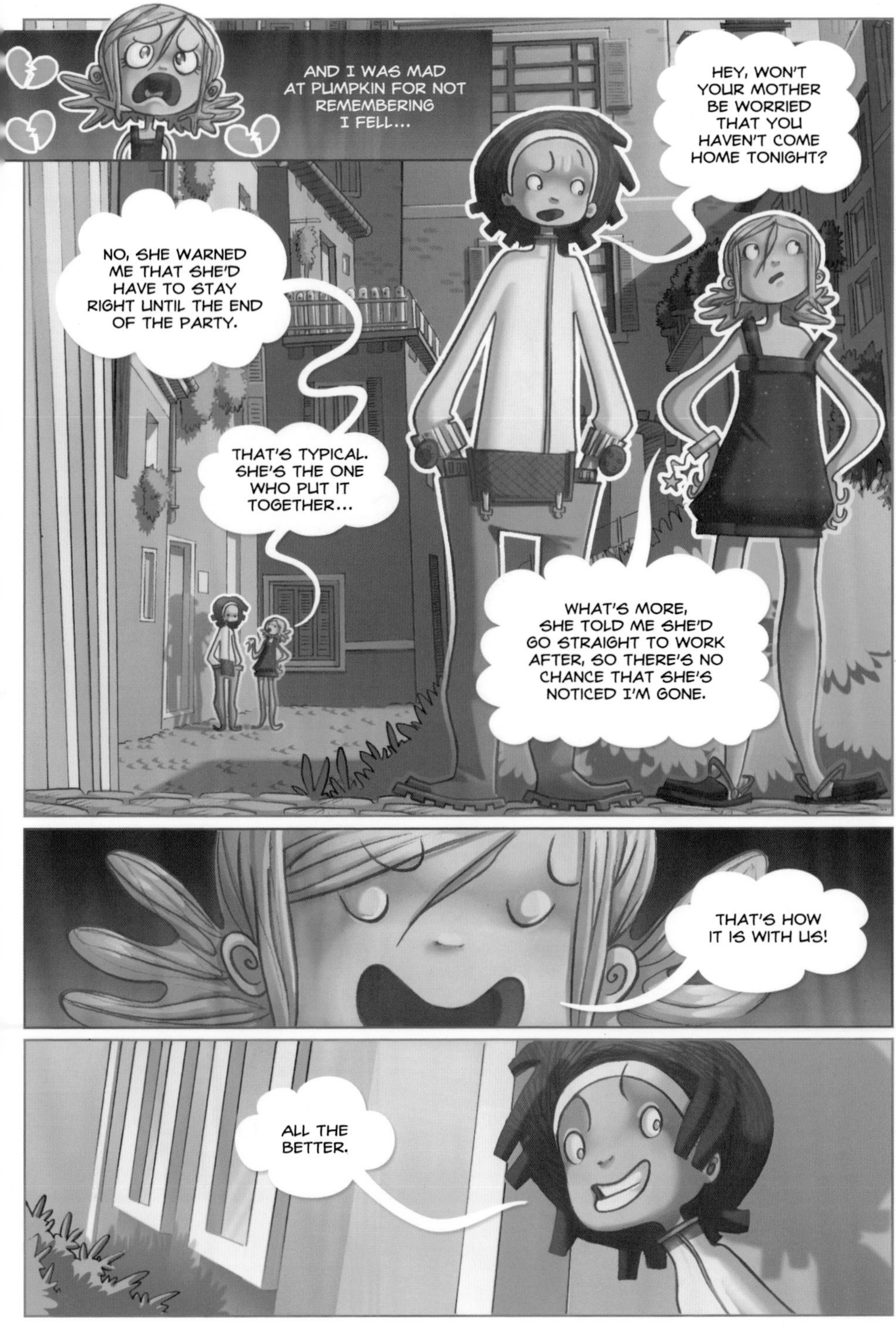
AND I WAS MAD AT PUMPKIN FOR NOT REMEMBERING I FELL...
HEY, WON'T YOUR MOTHER BE WORRIED THAT YOU HAVEN'T COME HOME TONIGHT?
NO, SHE WARNED ME THAT SHE'D HAVE TO STAY RIGHT UNTIL THE END OF THE PARTY.
THAT'S TYPICAL. SHE'S THE ONE WHO PUT IT TOGETHER...
WHAT'S MORE, SHE TOLD ME SHE'D GO STRAIGHT TO WORK AFTER, SO THERE'S NO CHANCE THAT SHE'S NOTICED I'M GONE.
THAT'S HOW IT IS WITH US!
ALL THE BETTER.

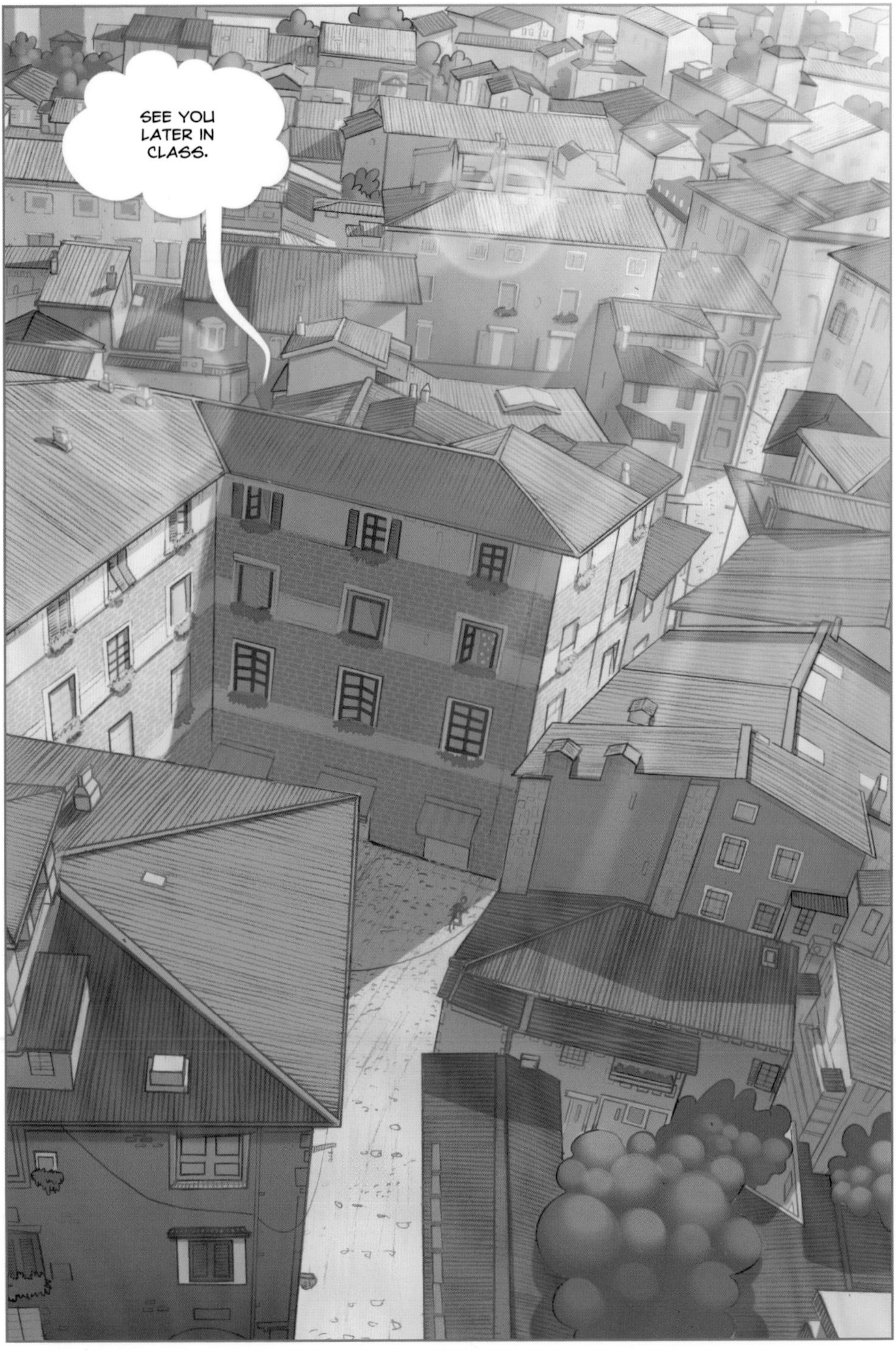
SEE YOU LATER IN CLASS.

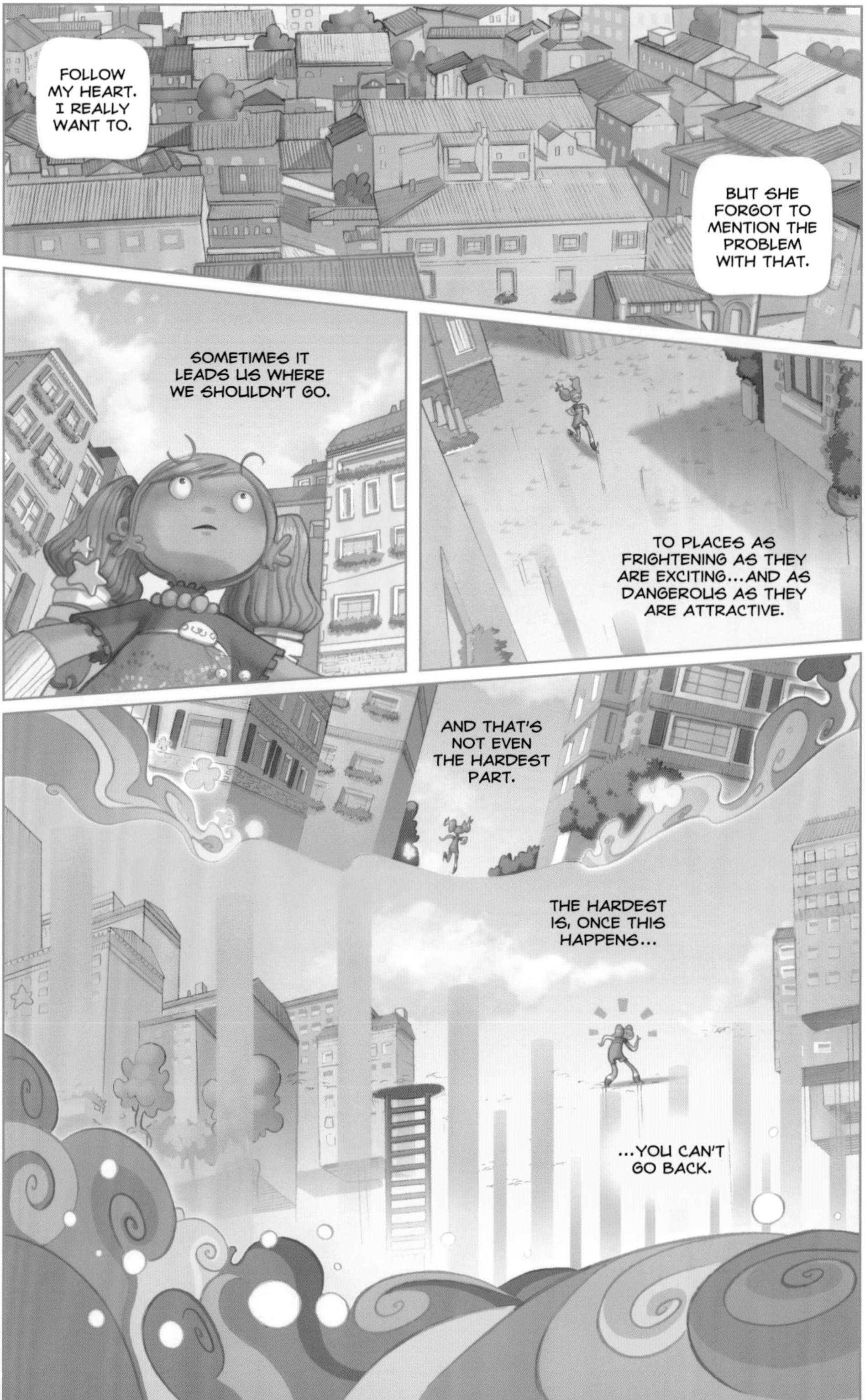
FOLLOW MY HEART. I REALLY WANT TO.
BUT SHE FORGOT TO MENTION THE PROBLEM WITH THAT.
SOMETIMES IT LEADS US WHERE WE SHOULDN'T GO.
TO PLACES AS FRIGHTENING AS THEY ARE EXCITING...AND AS DANGEROUS AS THEY ARE ATTRACTIVE.
AND THAT'S NOT EVEN THE HARDEST PART.
THE HARDEST IS, ONCE THIS HAPPENS...
...YOU CAN'T GO BACK.

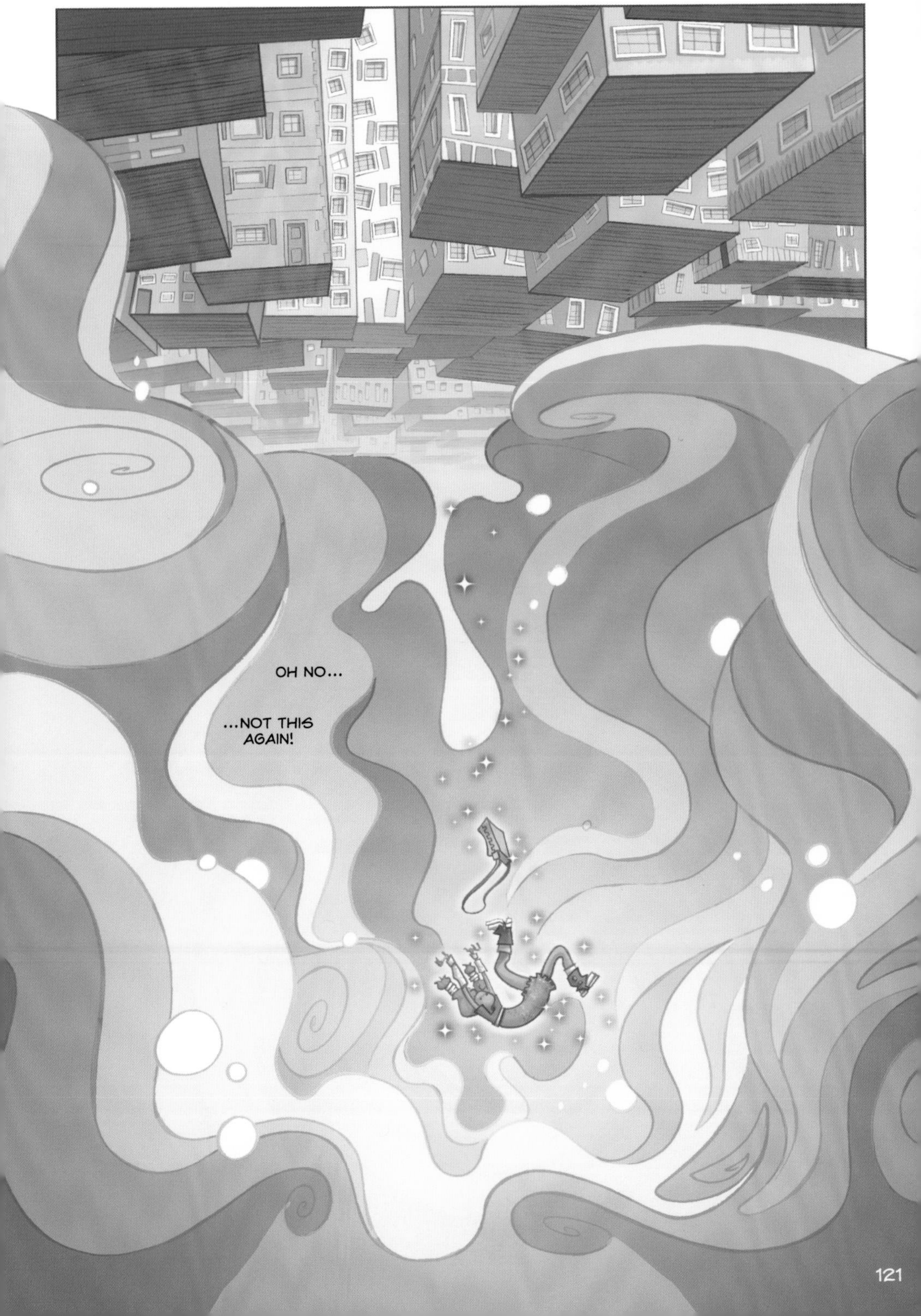
OH NO...
...NOT THIS AGAIN!

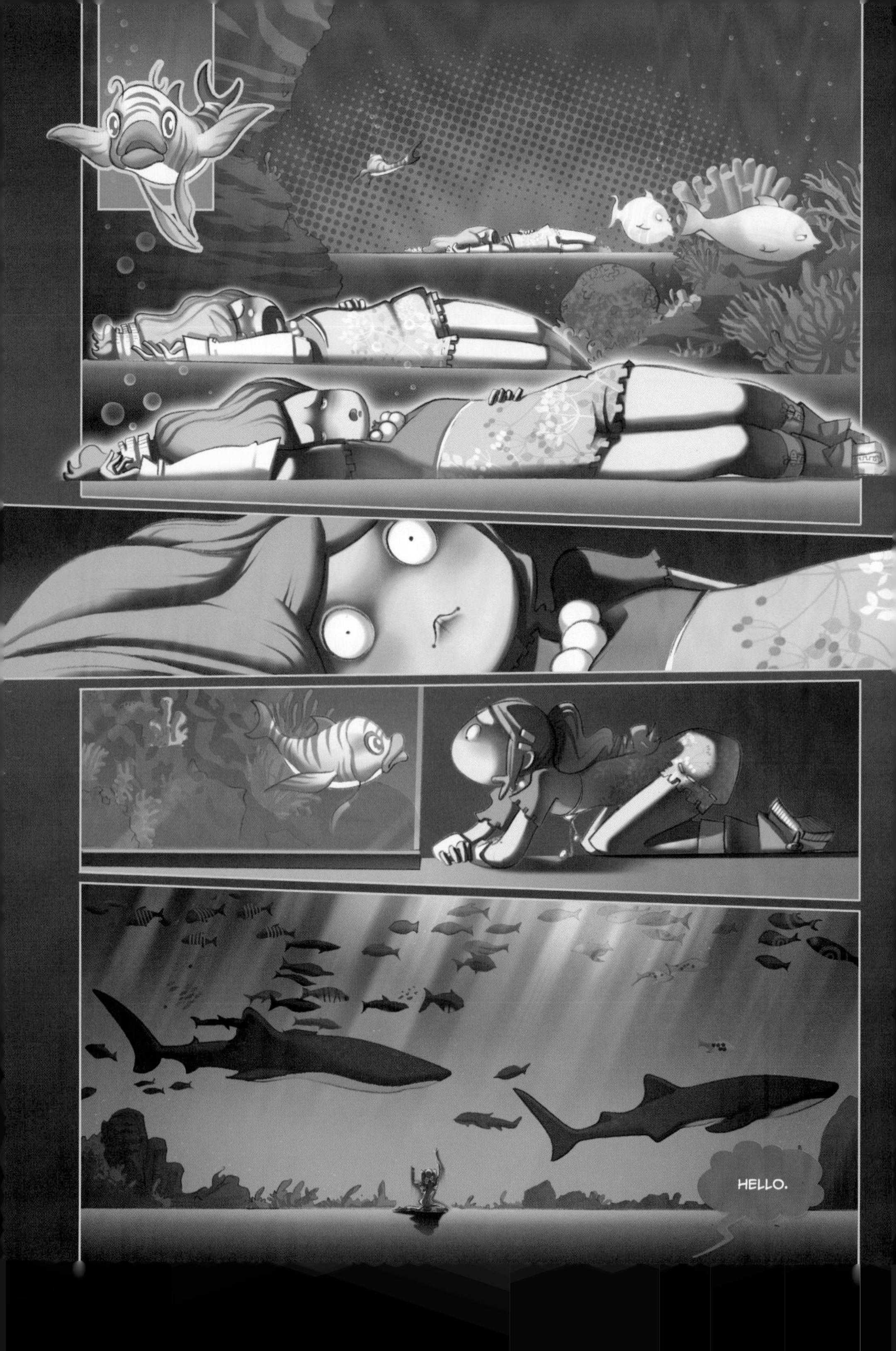
HELLO.

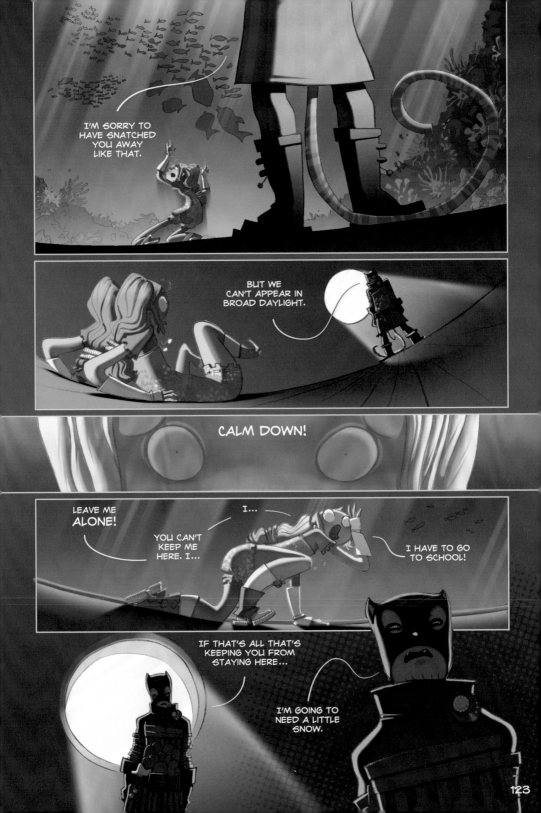

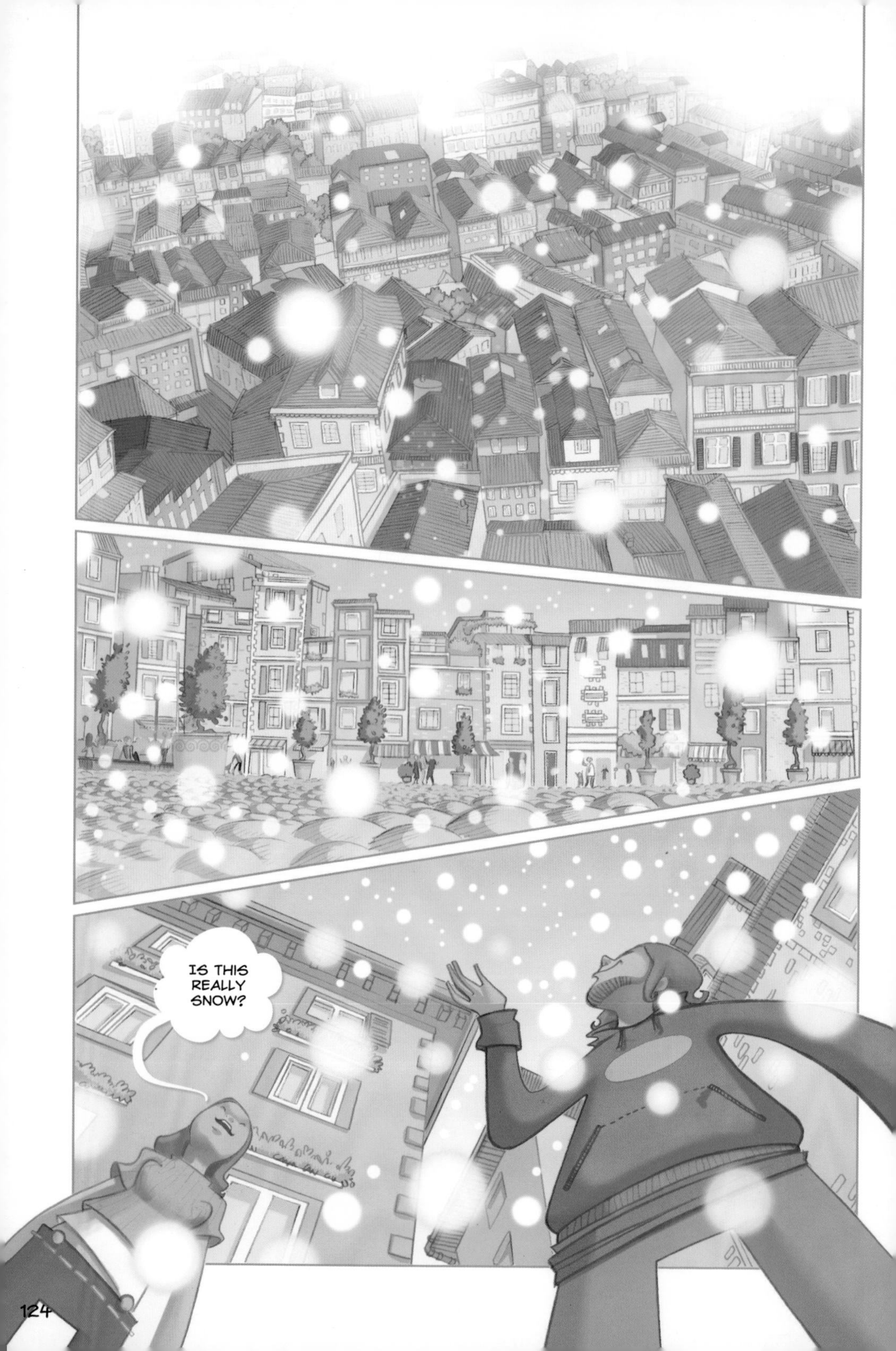
IS THIS REALLY SNOW?

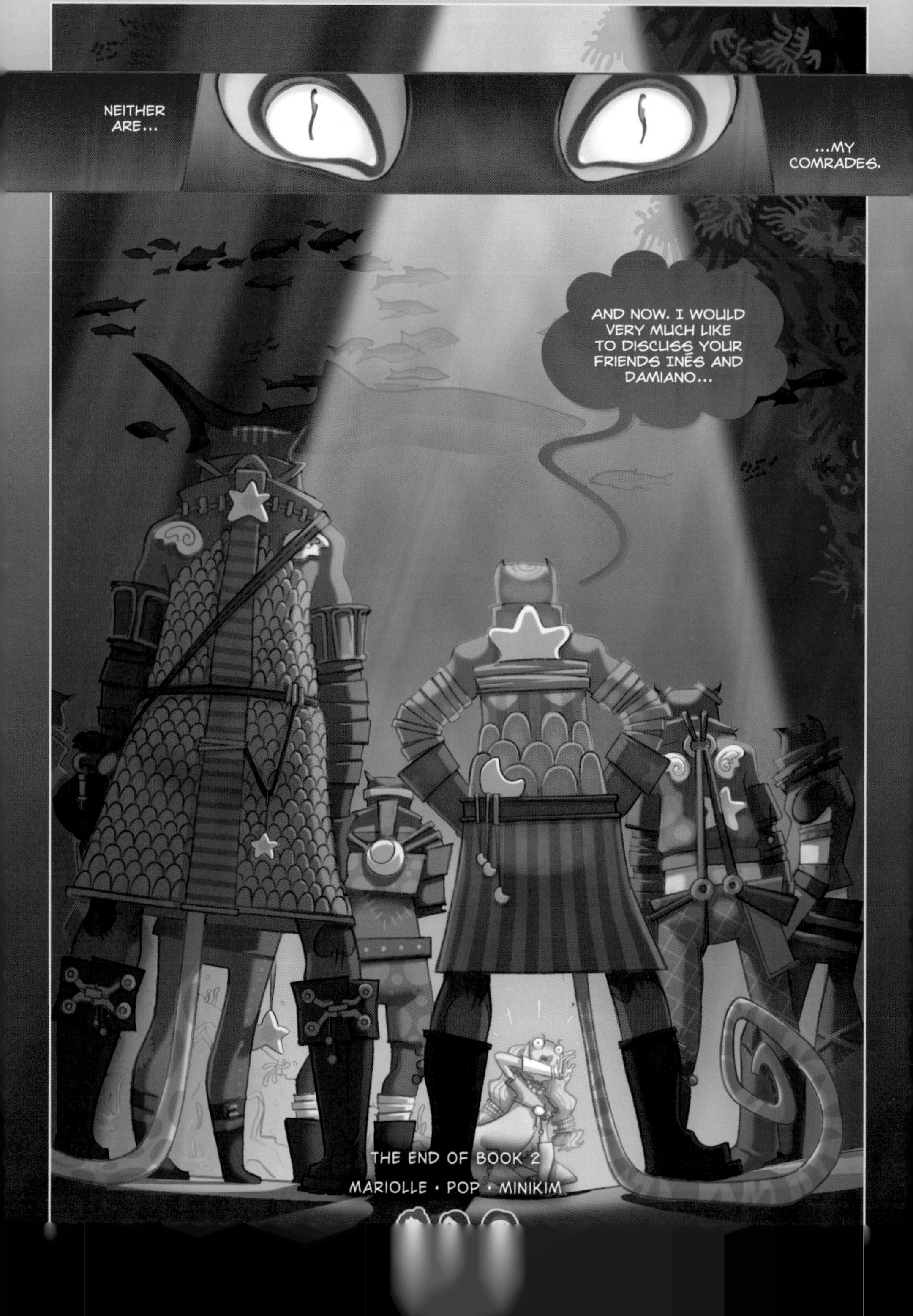
NEITHER ARE...
...MY COMRADES.
AND NOW. I WOULD VERY MUCH LIKE TO DISCUSS YOUR FRIENDS INÈS AND DAMIANO...
THE END OF BOOK 2
MARIOLLE • POP • MINIKIM

coming in Nola's Worlds #3...

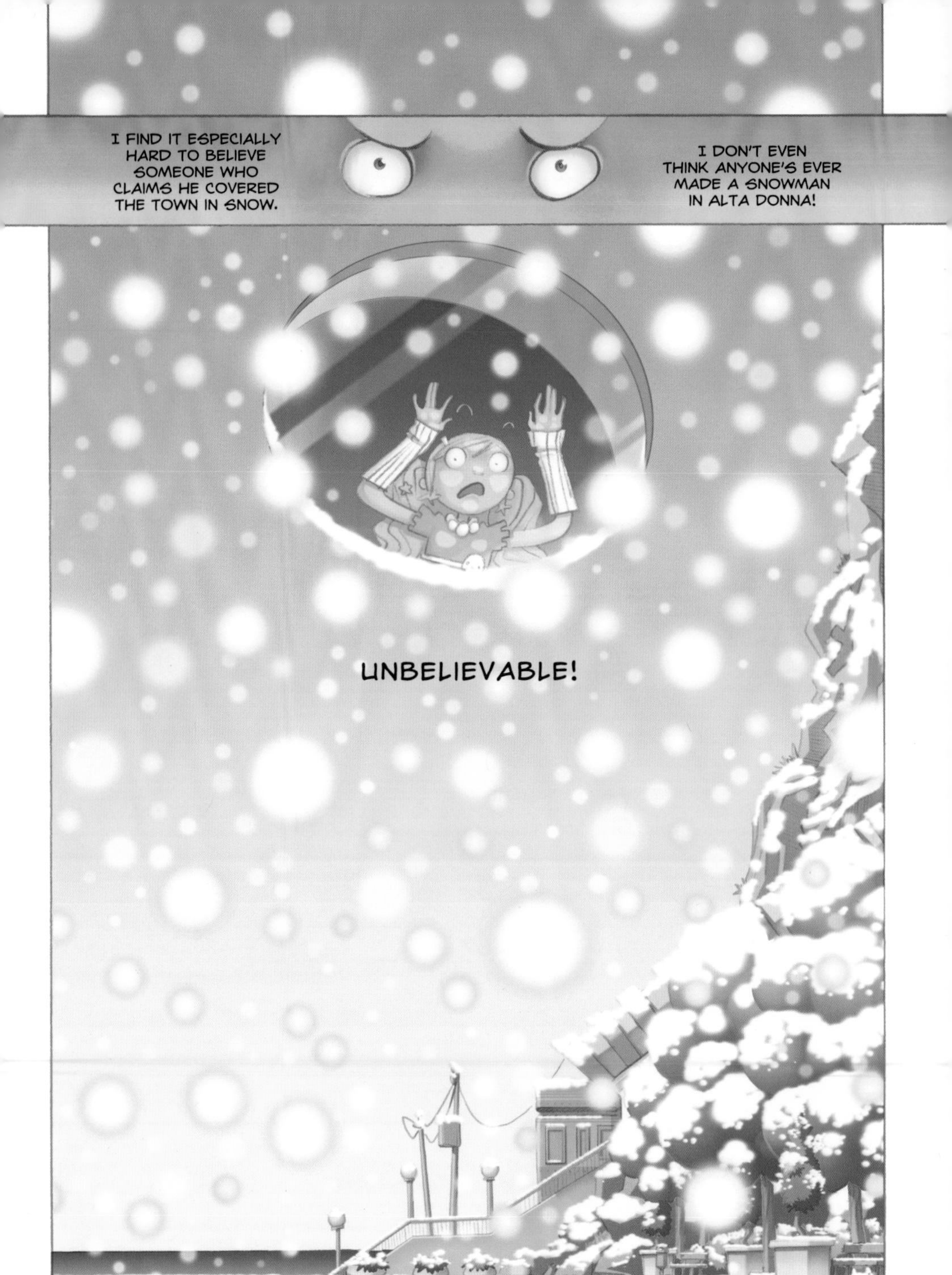
I FIND IT ESPECIALLY HARD TO BELIEVE SOMEONE WHO CLAIMS HE COVERED THE TOWN IN SNOW.
I DON'T EVEN THINK ANYONE'S EVER MADE A SNOWMAN IN ALTA DONNA!
UNBELIEVABLE!